I0788950

A SCIENCE FICTION
ALIEN INVASION STORY

THE LORDS OF SUMMER

REBELLION

TRISTAN VICK

A REGOLITH PUBLICATIONS BOOK

THE LORDS OF SUMMER: REBELLION
Book 4 in The Lords of Summer Series
A Dark Forces of Nature Novella
By Tristan Vick ©2025. All Rights Reserved
www.tristanvick.com

Published by Regolith Publications
First Edition, copyright © December 15, 2025.

Stock Art "Meteor Shower" by: Andy_Art @ Pixabay
Final chapter art by: Christopher Awayan
Cover design by: Regolith Design
Written & Edited by Tristan Vick

ISBN: 978-1-950106-19-6

Contents

1

REBELLION
PART 1: CHICAGO AT LAST

Seven days from first contact with a new alien species, seven days after surviving our first ever Hunter Killer alien encounter, and after a perilous escape from Woodridge High School, which we blew to high heaven along with several of the horrifying creatures, to five days on the dangerous road, we at long last had made it to Chicago.

We navigated the city, weaving up and down the city street s as we made our way to Northwest Memorial Hospital in search of my mother, Emily Rachelle Mahoney. And since our only clue as to any of our parents' whereabouts came from Mr. Anders, we had a lot riding on this.

Entering the city from the west, Jennifer Nakamura, dressed like a ninja right out of the Chuck Norris movie *Octagon*, showed us how to safely avoid the alien hives.

Following the Massacre at Make-Out Point, Jen told us the story of how she came to Chicago. After she assumed everyone had been killed, she had fled into the woods and ran back home, the alien hot on her heels. At some point during her mad-dash through the forest, it turned away, giving up its prey. Of course, unbeknownst to Jen, what had really happened is that the creature had caught our scent and, so, gave up its pursuit of her to come after us.

Coincidentally, Jen gave Sarah a chance to escape and, in turn, Sarah's run in with us attracted the creature and, likewise, gave Jen a chance to escape too. In a roundabout way, they saved each other.

Relatively unscathed from the alien encounter, apart from some scratches from running through the woods at night, Jen had made it home, where she cleaned her wounds and tried calling all of her friends. When there was no answer, she assumed the worst. Because she was panic stricken, however, she didn't think to call the cops. And, even if she had, they probably wouldn't have believed her. Not initially, anyway.

So, Jen told us she decided to take her parent's car to Chicago, where they were attending a medical conference. She knew the name of their hotel here parents were staying at—the Pendry Hotel downtown. So, she cleaned herself up, packed a bag, and drove all through the night, leaving behind the terror in the woods and a trail of dead bodies.

According to Jen, half a dozen buses had passed her on her way into town. They were heading away from the city, and she didn't realize until much later that these buses were probably evacuating people from downtown, which had turned into a veritable war zone between the cops, gangs, and aliens.

By the way Jen described the horrific events to us, it was clear to all of us that things were far worse than anything we'd seen thus far. The level of carnage made the Massacre at Make-Out Point look like a kid's movie by comparison. In fact, there hadn't been this level of needless death since two meteor strikes drilled their way through the city, bringing with it at least ten of the creatures and a level of death and destruction not seen since the Vietnam War.

While the police fought a losing battle, most of

the people fled the city. Others locked themselves inside their homes.

Meanwhile, many of the street gangs engaged the aliens, unleashing ungodly amounts of illegal firepower on the creature's from outer space. But the bigger creature's, the one's bigger than Lucy, had much thicker skin. And short of an elephant gun, nothing was going to take them down.

We'd seen this with the poachers too, because it took literally three men with machine guns and multiple rounds to take even one of the creatures down. Needless to say, from what Jen relayed, Chicago was a bloodbath for the first several days.

Thinning out the human resistance, more and more aliens naturally began to convene in and around the Chicago metro area. Jen told us that the radio theorized that they were using the beach as a breeding grounds. As such, more aliens were arriving by the day.

But even with the city completely overrun by extraterrestrial monsters, Jen risked entering the city to look for her parents.

"They weren't here?" Jimmy asked. He gave her a worried look and she lowered her gaze and shook her head solemnly.

"No," Jen replied. "I'm afraid not."

"That's too bad," Jimmy said, sympathizing with her tragic story. "So, what did you do?"

"When I got to the Pendry," she informed us, "I checked the ledger and found their room number. Luckily, I found a maid's cleaning cart with a master key and was able to enter the business suite. Once inside, I found a note."

"What kind of note?" I asked. I looked over at Jimmy and he nodded, because he wanted to know what it said too.

"It'll make more sense if I just read it to you." Jen reached into her cloak and then drew out a piece of paper. Unfolding it, she read it to us.

Jen, if you're reading this, your mom and I got on the evacuation shuttle out of the city. We don't know where they're taking us, but we'll contact you the moment we find out. Hopefully, you're still safe at home and won't ever see this message. But if you come searching for us, use the room and stay put until we can call you.

"That was seven days ago," she said, carefully folding the note back up and tucking it back inside her cloak.

"Now what?" Melody asked, scanning all of our faces.

"Now we look for mom," I said. Everyone nodded in agreement and we continued on our way into town.

As we walked straight to the business district we noticed there was an eerie quiet in the city. No traffic sounds, no cars honking, or police or ambulance sirens. There wasn't any construction going on. No beeping of Lorry trucks backing up or car alarms going off. No distant wail of babies crying and no dogs barking. Walking down the empty city streets was deathly silent.

It seemed, by our account, that the Hunter Killer aliens had made good work of the city. According to Jennifer Nakamura, we needed to avoid Soldier Field at all costs. The stadium, she warned us, was where the main hive was and was guarded by at least fifty or sixty aliens while another dozen patrolled a three block radius around the stadium.

That's where the hive was, Jen told us. She mentioned that she'd seen the aliens seek out soft ground so that they could burrow into the earth, and lay giant reptilian styled eggs. As much as we all wanted to see the eggs for ourselves, we didn't want to risk ticking off the aliens. So, we stayed on course until we were in sight of the Hospital

The spire of the hospital's tallest tower could be seen from several blocks away. What we hadn't expected, though, was the twenty-foot tall, all concrete barricade that walled off that section of town.

"Ah, man," Jimmy groaned. "How are we supposed to get past that? It must be fifty feet tall."

"More like twenty or thirty feet, actually," Billy interjected, correcting Jimmy's wild estimate.

"Like I said," Jimmy replied, revising his original assessment since the last thing he wanted was to seem like a complete idiot. "That thing must be at least twenty feet tall. Maybe thirty."

We all stood in front of the twenty foot concrete wall and peered up at the top. The top had overhanging razor barbed wire bolted to it, so even if you did get up to the top, you'd need wire cutters to get through without being maimed by the razor-wire.

"It's a pickle, that's for sure," I said.

"A pickle?" asked Megan. She put her hands on her hips and shot me a curious glance.

"Yeah," I replied, "as in a sticky wicket."

"What are you talking about?"

"You've never heard the phrase... oh, never mind," I said. "It's not important."

"Between a rock and a hard place," Billy informed Megan, helping me clarify precisely what I meant.

I snapped my fingers and pointed at him. "Yes. That." Turning to Megan, I shot her a sly grin. "See, Billy gets it."

"Don't mind him," Melody said, coming to Megan's defense. "He always talks like he's from the 1930s."

"Jen," Sarah said, turning toward miss Nakamura. "You said you have a hotel room?"

"Yeah," replied Jen.

"Does it have running water?" Megan asked.

"Yes. Surprisingly enough, everything in the city still works."

Sarah turned toward us all and then said, "I vote we go change, take hot baths, get clean and maybe change out of these clothes."

"I am a little ripe," Jimmy said, sniffing his armpits.

"A little?" Melody balked.

"Be nice," I said. "We're all on the sour side. Personally, I think Sarah is right. We haven't had a bath since the farm house. And that was five days ago."

Jen turned back toward downtown and said, "In that case, follow me." She then glanced over her shoulder at us and added, "But stay close. The aliens send scouts out on patrol every few hours."

"Why?" asked Jimmy. "Why would they do that?"

"To kill any humans they find," Jen replied. She then looked over at Lucy, or rather, she glared at Lucy.

Sif barked and trotted up the road, then turned around and barked at us again.

"If Sif says it's safe," Jen said, "Then we're in the clear. But Sif will be the first to sense something is off, so pay close attention to her."

We all nodded and started to follow Sif up the road. Before we'd broken away from the wall, however, Jen turned to Melody and said, "I'm afraid it's going to have to stay behind." Jen pointed her chin at Lucy and Melody nodded, showing she understood.

Touching her little head to her pet alien's forehead, Melody placed both hands on his massive temples and whispered, "I'm sorry, boy. But you've gotta stay out here, with your kind. We'll meet again soon. I promise."

Lucy huffed and then sat down and watched us head up the road. I waved goodbye as we parted ways. Although Lucy and my sister definitely shared a telepathic connection of some kind, I too had linked minds with Lucy and was beginning to feel comfortable with him.

I knew that if we could understand the aliens, then maybe we could live in harmony with them. Right now, all the killing was instinct based. As far as any of us could tell, there wasn't any motive behind it other than survival. And, if they were smart, like elephants or even dogs, then maybe the killing could finally come to an end, and we'd eventually be able to rebuild our towns and our cities.

By the sounds of things, the aliens were building a hive network, not so unlike ants or bees, where they'd lay and hatch eggs. How many young could Lucy's kind produce? If it was a few dozen, then there'd be no problem. If it was a few hundred, or a few thousand, then we were royally screwed.

We'd cross that bridge when we came to it. Right now, we simply needed to get to the Pendry Hotel. And, about forty five minutes later, we arrived at the classic art-deco styled building.

Riding the elevator to the thirty-third floor of the building, Jen let us into her hotel suite, 72A. Once we entered, we threw all our things into a pile in the living room area and gave ourselves a quick tour of the place.

"Hey," Melody said, excitedly as she poked her head into the master bathroom. "They have a jacuzzi bathtub.

We all looked at one another, glancing back and forth, and everyone seemed to be on the exact same page. Sarah, Megan, Billy, Jimmy, and my sister all began peeling off layers of soiled clothes until they were down to their underwear.

Jen looked over at me and I turned my head, noting the bewildered look on her face.

"Oh, right," I said. "You weren't with us. Uh, we

found a hot tub a few days back and found it was easier to bathe together than separately. I dropped my gear and then pulled my shirt off over my head. Then, turning to Jen, I asked, "Care to join us?"

"Did I mention you people were crazy?" she said, eyeing me suspiciously. Then, a bright smile breaking across her lips, she said, "Why not?"

Jen followed after me, shedding her clothes as she made her way down the hallway. It was no surprise that she had on black matching underwear with a satin finish. Of all the girls, Jen was perhaps the most luxurious in both style and look. You could tell her parents had money. Real money. Which made sense, since they were both doctors.

Sif, meanwhile, was in seventh heaven amid a sea of our dirty clothes and ran to one pile of discarded clothing to the next, sniffing every single pile with that excitable dog energy that makes our fluffy companions so delightful. Eventually, she curled up on a little nest she'd made of our dirty clothes and fell fast asleep.

Once we'd convened in the super luxurious master bathroom with encaustic tiled floors, golden lighting fixtures that gave the room a warm glow, we all piled into the massive jacuzzi. It overflowed, since there were too many of us, and we laughed together while Billy, Jen, and I sat on the edge of the tub while everyone else soaked away their concerns.

"So," Jen said, glancing around at all our faces. "Is this it? We just sit here in our underwear and bathe?"

"If that's too boring for you, we could skinny dip!" Jimmy offered. He smiled at Jen and wiggled his ginger eyebrows at her. This caused her to give him a double take but she shook her head.

His suggestion, however, was met with a resounding, "No thanks!" from Sarah, Megan, and my sister, who all blurted it out simultaneously. Megan even splashed water into his face causing him to cough and choke on it.

"It got in my mouth," he said, still coughing.

We all laughed some more and Jen leaned over and nudged me with her bare shoulder. This spiked a look of jealousy from Megan who, to her credit, didn't say anything out of fear of being too catty. Regardless, she watched Jen like a Hawk.

Jen laughed. "You guys really are crazy. I love it."

"Not crazy," Billy said. "But we've been through so much together that, well, I think we're closer to family now than friends."

"I second that," Sarah said. She and Billy shared a glance of affection and deep seated friendship that could prove to anyone who bore witness that blood was thicker than water. That's a feeling we all shared. We might not be family by blood, but we were family nonetheless.

"You know what's strange," Jen said. We gave her inquisitive looks and she put her arms on the edge of the jacuzzi and leaned back, giving her hair a slight toss so that it brushed my shoulder. I glanced over at Megan whose eyes narrowed. "This brings me back to my summers in Japan, when we'd visit my grandparents."

"That's so cool," Jimmy said, showing a limerent level of interest in Jen's story. "I've always wanted to go to Japan!"

She smiled at him and continued on with her story. "One thing they wanted us to experience was bathing at the local *Onsen.*"

"Onsen?" asked Melody.

"It's the Japanese word for hot spring. Japan is a volcanic island, like Hawaii, and has a ton of natural hot springs all over the place. Japanese people have been turning these hot springs into communal bathing houses for centuries. The only difference is that, in Japan, you bathe totally naked."

"You get naked with strangers?" asked Melody as she folded her arms across her chest and shook her head. The look on her face wasn't quite one of disgust, but it was close. "No thank you."

Jen laughed again. "It's strange at first, I admit. But you get used to it."

"I don't think I'd be able to get used to it," Sarah said. "I mean, nothing against your culture, Jen. But it's not for me."

"I totally get that," Jen replied. She laughed again and tossed her long dark hair. Her hair brushed my shoulder and hit my face. It caused me to almost sneeze because it tickled my nose, but I managed to stifle the sneeze.

Glancing over at Megan again, I could see she was growing increasingly jealous of Jen by the minute as the green-eyed monster slowly overcame her. Naturally, I knew I needed to diffuse the situation lest she leap across the jacuzzi and strangle Jennifer with her bare hands.

"So, uh..." I cleared my throat and looked at Jen,

"What do you have to eat around here?"

"Yeah," Jimmy asked, sitting upright as he turned to Jen. "I'm starving."

With all eyes on her, Jen tapped her chin and thought about it for a moment. "Well, let me think." She gave it a moment and then a big smile broke across her face. "My parents stocked the fridge with food. Oh, and we have steaks in the freezer."

"Steaks?" Billy asked, his interesting now piquing. "Did I hear you correctly? You have steak?"

"Steaks," she reiterated. "As in all you can eat."

Suddenly, somebody's stomach growled, making all kinds of gurgling noises and my sis' covered her tummy and said, "Sorry. I guess I'm hungry too."

"That settles it then," Jen said, standing up right next to me. I looked over at her and then immediately looked away realizing where my eyeline was. Luckily, Megs didn't hold it against me. "We'll get dried off and cook up some steaks."

"What about our clothes?" Sarah asked.

"Oh, that's no problem," Jen said as she walked over and grabbed a pristine white Egyptian cotton towel from the towel rack. "The hotel has a dry cleaning service downstairs. And everyone left in such a hurry, there's a ton of clothes you could wear."

Jen dabbed her chest, making a show of it, which tantalized Jimmy for sure, then smiled at me and tossed me the towel. The towel hit me in my face and I reflexively caught it. Jimmy drew up next to me and I quickly handed off the towel to him.

"Here," I said, practically stuffing it into his hands.

"She's so dreamy," he said.

"I'll, uh, take your word for it," I replied. I looked over at Megs who was about to lunge across the tile floor and claw Jen to death if not for Sarah holding her back.

"Don't let her get to you," Sarah said. "We all know Jen is the class flirt."

"More like class slut," Megan said under her breath.

Luckily, Jen didn't hear her snide remark and we all filed out of the tub and dried off.

All of our stomachs seemed to synch up, because they all gurgled and gargled at the same time, as though they were communicating with each other, and we all had a good laugh.

"Let's get them steaks," Jen said. She spun

around and walked out of the bathroom, swaying her hips as she went.

"Hottest babe on the planet," Jimmy said.

"You might want to wipe the drool from your face, Cassanova," Melody quipped as she walked by.

Jimmy merely smacked his lips and then wiped the actual drool from his mouth with the back of his hand.

"You've got it bad, man," I said, shooting Jimmy with a slightly worried look.

"I know," Jimmy replied. "I think I'm in love."

2

REBELLION
PART 2: A LITTLE DOWN TIME

AFTER OUR LITTLE SHOPPING SPREE IN THE Pendry Hotel's storage room, we managed to find clothes that fit us. Not only that, but the clothes were much fancier than our regular school clothes and we all looked like a bunch of super rich prep kids.

Once everyone arrived back at Jen's hotel suite on the thirty-third floor, we got out the steaks and began cooking. Billy, wore his new tight fitting black Metallica t-shirt, and Megs, who wore pink sweatpants and a white tank top, helped him cook the steaks. Meanwhile, Melody, in her blue jeans and yellow half sleeve t-shirt, and Sarah, who had on a light blue halter top and denim shorts, boiled and mashed potatoes.

I found a burgundy t-shirt and khaki pants and was buttering bread to toast in the oven, a trick my mom showed me with garlic toast. Baking the toast in the oven let you make larger quantities for when you had lots of company, during something like Thanksgiving or birthday parties.

While I worked on that, Jennifer Nakamura came over to me wearing a yellow, backless summer dress and white leather Gogo boots. "So, what's the deal with you and Powerhouse over there?" She leaned on the end of the counter and nodded her head in the general direction of Megan.

Megan was in the middle of laughing at something Billy had said when she turned to see Jen talking to me. Her eyes narrowed and although Billy was telling her something amusing, she merely nodded and stared menacingly at Jen.

"I mean, she's been giving me the evil eye ever since we got to the hotel."

"Oh," I said, looking down into the bowl as I tossed salad. I was pretty much finished making the salad, but I didn't want to seem over interested in Jen, seeing as she kept singling me out. "I think she's just being overprotective of me."

"You're not her brother though, right?"

"Who me?" I laughed. "No."

"Oh, I thought she had a brother."

"She does," I informed her. "Mitch. But he stayed back in Woodridge with our friend Paul and his family."

"Oh," Jen replied, more confused than when she began. "So, why is she protective of you again?"

"Because we're dating," I replied. I looked up and by the look on Jen's face, I could tell she didn't believe me.

"You?" she laughed, unable to believe her ears. "Are you telling me that Megan the Powerhouse McIntyre and you are a thing?"

"Yeah," I replied. "Why is that funny?"

"She's like five ten. You're barely five seven."

"Five foot eight," I corrected.

"Whatever. My point is, she could eat you alive."

"What makes you think I wouldn't like that?" I said, grinning coyly.

Jen laughed again. "Oh, I see how it is. You're a big pervert."

"No," I said, shaking my head and looking back down at the salad greens. "I just really like her. That's all."

Jen leaned forward and touched my forearm.

"And if I keep flirting with you, do you think I can get a rise out of her?"

When I looked up again, Megs was suddenly standing beside Jen. "Hey, Jen," Megan said. Jen swiveled her head and smiled at Megan.

"Oh, hey there, Megs. What's up?"

Megan calmly reached down and grabbed Jen's wrist, lifted it off my arm, and then set it down onto the counter. "Could you please get your grubby mitts off of my boyfriend?"

Jen took a step back and her eyes widened with surprise. "Wow. So, you two really are dating?"

We nodded and Jen shook her head.

"I'm so sorry," she apologized. "I thought he was just stringing me along. You know how guys are, they'll make stuff up about how hot their girlfriend is to try and trick you into being more interested in them because they want you to think that they're some kind of great catch."

"You thought I was stringing you along?" I asked. "Why?"

"I, uh…" Jen looked at me then Megan and then me again. "I don't know. I just thought maybe… you liked me?"

"Please don't take this the wrong way, Jen," I said. "But I don't have any feelings for you either way. Jimmy is the one who's got the hots for you."

"Jimmy?" Jen asked. "Which one is he again?"

She threw her hands on her hips and turned to look at everyone.

Megan and I stood beside her and we turned to look too, but there was no sign of Jimmy. "Um, that's a good question," I replied.

"Hey, guys," Megan said. "Have any of you seen our resident bone-head, Jimbo anywhere?"

"Yeah," Sarah replied. "He was having trouble deciding what to wear and mentioned that he was going to hang back and try on several outfits."

"Do you think we should check on him?" I asked.

"No need," Melody said. She pointed her ladle at the room entrance and we all spun around to see Jimmy standing in the doorway wearing a pin stripe suit and sporting a fedora.

Sif, who was sitting at the foot of the sofa, sat up and barked. "Woof!"

"What in the world?" I asked.

"You look like a 1930's gangster," Megan said. "Which is to say, ridiculous."

"Ridicule all you want, kid," Jimmy replied, speaking like Al Capone. "But you'll never have half the style I do, see?" With that, he took his jacket off, flung it over his shoulder, and spun around. He even had on suspenders.

Billy laughed. "You look like a dork. A stylish dork maybe. But a dork all the same."

"Fair enough," Jimmy said with a shrug. He took off his had and hung both the hat and jacket on the wall-hook styled coat hanger next to the entrance.

"Just get washed up and help us finish making the gravy. Then we can all eat," Sarah said. "Oh, and Jimbo… I think you look pretty slick."

Getting a compliment like that from Sarah Lewis, of all people, was a big deal. Jimmy's eyes widened and his head perked up. "You really think so?"

"Sure do."

Jimmy sauntered over to us and, leaning into Megs, said, "Hear that, doll face? Your friend thinks I'm slick. Real slick."

"The only thing around here that will be slick are my fists after I bash in your brains, smartass," Megan replied, leaning forward as she was about to walk over to him and pummel him.

Not wanting my friend to be beaten to death by my girlfriend, I intercepted her and held her back. She just grabbed onto me and pretended to lunge at Jimmy as I held her back.

Jimmy flinched and leaned back, giving himself the maximum distance from her bodacious brand of crazy. "Everyone's a critic," he said, adjusting his necktie.

"Sarah's not wrong," Jen said. "You look real slick." She smiled at Jimmy then turned and walked over to Melody to help her make the gravy.

"Did you hear that?" Jimmy said, settling back into his regular sounding voice. "She thinks I'm slick."

The hotel suite had a dining room with a table that could hold six comfortably and seven or eight if you squeezed in tight. For us, it was perfect.

We ate, we laughed, we each took turns making fun of Jimmy's suit. But after our bellies were full and our spirits lifted, Sarah went into the kitchen and then came back with a bottle of white sparkling champagne. She popped the cork, held up the bottle, and made an announcement.

"Given everything we've been through, I think we should celebrate," she said." We held out our glasses and she poured champagne for each of us. As she filled our cups, she added, "I don't condone underage drinking. But, at the same time, I think we've earned it."

Once our cups were full, Megan sounded off, raising her wine glass. "To friends. To family!"

We raised our cups too, clinked them together, and said, "Here, here!" Then everyone took a big swig of the bubbly stuff.

Hacking and coughing instantly ensued.

"This stuff is vile!" Melody said, spitting hers out.

"Gross," Jimmy said, his face contorting into all kinds of sour looks.

"It really is…a special kind of terrible…" I added.

Sarah swallowed but then dumped her glass into the sink. "Yeah. I thought that would be better."

Megan simply set her glass down and slid it away from herself. "Who knew alcohol tasted so bad?"

"It's not that bad," Jen said. We all turned to her as she sipped daintily from her glass. When she realized we were all staring at her, she paused and said, somewhat defensively, "What?"

"How can you drink that stuff?" Jimmy asked. "It tastes like sour grapes plucked out of a sweaty ass."

"I don't know," Jen replied. "My parents have always let my brother and I have a glass now and then."

"Like on holidays?" I asked.

"No," Jen replied. "Weekends. Trips to the cabin in Aspin. Holidays, of course. But, also, non-holidays. You know, basically whenever."

"So, you're like an alcoholic?" asked Melody.

Jen paused and thought about it for a moment, then shrugged. "Maybe."

"Even so," Jimmy stated, "She's still the hottest girl here. No offense, ladies." He looked over at Sarah and Megan.

"No offense taken, dickweed," Megan replied. She flipped him the bird and Sarah laughed and reached over and pushed Megan's arm back down to her side.

"You're fine, Jimbo," Sarah replied.

Jen was already pouring herself another drink when there was a loud boom that shook the whole building. We all jumped in fright and spun to look out the windows. In the distance, we could see heavy artillery lighting up the night sky.

"What in the blazes is that?" asked Billy, walking over to the windows.

"Best you stay away from the windows," Jen said. "The military periodically engages with the aliens when they get too... how shall I put this, um, friendly."

"Friendly?"

"As in the aliens try to break inside the base to kill all humans kind of friendly."

"And they built the base around the hospital?" asked Sarah.

"It was the logical place to make a stand," Jen answered. "Don't worry though, they never come over this way. The aliens I mean."

"Good to know," Melody said. "Now, I think I'm going to go find one of the big beds to sleep in." She stood up and, looking over at Sif, called out, "Come here, girl."

Sif jumped off the sofa and followed Melody into the bedroom.

"I think my sister has the right idea," I said. "We

could all use a good sleep. In the morning, we find mom."

Megan put her hand on my shoulder and gave an affectionate squeeze. I cover her hand with mine, and looked into her ocean blue eyes.

"I'll stay with Melody and Sif in the king-sized bed," Sarah informed us. She stifled a yawn and then waved goodnight as she headed to bed.

"I guess the rest of us will sleep in the living room area," Billy said.

"I call dibs by the fireplace," Jimmy stated.

"Megs and I will take the couch," I added.

"That leaves the floor for you and me, handsome," Jen said, leaning over and shooting Billy a seductive glance. She then let out an obnoxiously loud burp and poured herself her fourth glass of champagne.

Billy intercepted the glass just as she was about to take another swill of the bubbly stuff and said, "Maybe we slow down with the champagne."

He set the glass over on the edge of the counter by the sink. Jen stood up, swayed slightly as she scanned the room, and then said, "Hey, I was drinking that."

"You can have more tomorrow," Billy replied.

She seemed to be satisfied with that answer and then swiveled around to head to her bedroom only to see through the open door that her bed was full. "Oh, poop. I have no place to sleep."

She belched again and wiped her lips with the back of her hand as she swayed like a branch in the wind. She slowly turned back toward the rest of us and watched everyone from behind her inebriated haze. It seemed like she was waiting for someone to say something and Jimmy was the first to break the silence.

"You can sleep on this fancy rug next to me," Jimmy said.

Jen sighed. "Fine, I'll sleep next to the fire and the ginger."

I unpacked Sarah's sleeping bag for Jen and laid it out for her. She smiled at me and touched my hand with hers, prompting Megan to lean over and slap her hand away.

"Ow," Jen said, reeling her hand back in to her body. She looked over at Megan with a sly grin.

"We've talked about this," Megan said.

Jen giggled. "Sorry."

Not taking it personally, Jen turned around and mumbled in slurred fashion, "I have to pee, help me get this dress off." She turned toward Jimmy and the fireplace, her back to us, and unzipped the back of her dress, and pulled it down to her waist.

When Jimmy realized Jen wasn't wearing any bra, his eyes grew to the size of saucers. Standing topless in front of Jimmy, she stumbled forward on wobbly legs and fell into his arms. As he held her, he looked over her shoulder at us, frozen in fear, and mouthed the words, "What do I do?"

"Enjoy the drunk girl, Jimbo," Megan said. "Because in the morning she'll regret every choice. But, as you can clearly see, she'll have earned it."

"Come on now," I said, taking Megan's hand in mine. "Let's not be mean."

"She's a boyfriend stealing floozy!" Megan shouted. "And she's smashed out of her gourd."

"Hey," a voice said. Megs and I turned to see Jen's finger pointed directly at Megan's face. I also happened to notice she was facing us, girls out in the wild and everything.

"Whoa, there," I said, shielding my eyes. But, of course, I still peeked through my fingers. I mean, who wouldn't? "You might want to put those away."

"Hey, did you just...?" When Megs glanced over at me and noticed me peeking, she punched my shoulder. Hard.

"Ouch!" I exclaimed, rubbing my arm. "Okay, I might have deserved that."

"You're damn right you deserved that," Megs said. Then, turning toward Jen, she let out a sigh and put her arm across Jen's shoulder, using her body to shield Jen's nudity from our prying eyes.

"Hey, sweetie, how about we put those puppies away?" Megan helped Jen back into her dress and Jen nodded and smiled.

Dressed, again, Jen reached up and, with slurred words, said, "You're really kind a sexy when you're angry." She then *booped* Megan's nose and proceeded to pass out. Jen fell into Megan's arms, who caught her and saved her from cracking her head on the fireplace mantle.

Megs rolled her eyes. "Uh, thanks, I guess?" Cradling Jen like a baby, she set Jen onto the sleeping bag next to Jimmy, who was sitting and watching events unfold with an amused half-grin on his face.

"I know she's drunk," Megan said, eyeballing

Jimbo. "But you keep your little pervy hands to yourself. If you so much as touch her while she's asleep, I'll tear your nuts off your peewee-sized dick and feed them to you."

Jimmy gulped loudly. "Understood," he replied. Then, crawling into his own sleeping bag, he did his best to try and get some sleep with a veritable goddess sleeping next to him.

"Well, that's about all the excitement I can handle for one evening," Billy said. He laid down on his sleeping bag and Megs and I, still holding hands, went and snuggled up on the couch.

Soon, a sonorous snoring filled the room and, like the white-noise of a humming refrigerator or the gentle whirring of a fan on a hot summer night, the steady rhythmic tones soothed and calmed us, lulling us into a deep sleep.

Come morning, I sat up and stretched. Looking around the room, I noticed that Billy and Jimmy were still fast asleep, but Jen was sitting legs crossed, as she sat perched on the living room coffee table. She had her eyes closed, her elbows resting on her knees, her fingertips pinched together.

"What are you doing?" I whispered.

Without opening her eyes, Jen took in a deep breath and, after holding it for a bit, exhaled slowly. "I'm meditating."

"Meditating about what?"

"What?" she asked, opening her eyes. She looked right at me.

"What?" I asked, having confused myself.

"It's not like dreaming," she answered, realizing what it was that I was trying to ask. "It's about clearing your mind. The key is to try and quiet your thoughts until there's nothing left to think or worry about. It's about letting go of those random pervasive thoughts that distract you. By allowing the world around you to fall away, you can find your center and come back in tune with your surroundings."

"Is that even possible?" I asked.

She closed her eyes and smiled. "It is."

I watched her meditate for a while and then realized that she was wearing pink sweats and a white tank top. The exact same outfit as Megan.

What in the world? I thought. That's strange.

Megan sat up on the sofa, yawned and then brushed my arm with her hand. I turned and smiled at her and when I did, she caught a glimpse of

Jennifer Nakamura and stood up.

"What the Hell is this best-friend Barbie and Midge nonsense?"

"What's what?" I asked.

Megan pointed at Jen, observing her pink sweats and white top, and then herself. "Why are you wearing the exact same outfit as me?!"

"Oh," Jen said with a laugh. "I hadn't noticed." She then looked right at me and mouthed silently, "I totally noticed."

Megan's little outburst roused Jimmy and Billy from their sleep and they both sat up.

"I've gotta piss like a race horse," Jimmy informed us as he stretched and let out a lengthy yawn.

"To much information, Cassanova," Megan said. Jimmy merely shrugged, passed us, and scratched his ass on his way to the bathroom.

Without warning the bedroom doors slammed open, and a frantic looking Sarah Lewis stood beneath the threshold panting heavily. "Travis," she said, leaning on the door sill as she attempted to catch her breath. "Your sister... She's..."

"Let me guess," I said, my whole day suddenly

ruined. "She's gone."

"Not again," lamented Jimmy. "This is the exact same thing she did that morning when she ran off to Fort Liberty to feed her stupid alien Kit Kat bars."

On that note, Megs and I looked at one another at the exact same time, and said, "Lucy!"

"Lucy?" Jen asked, breaking her meditation and scooting off the coffee table. "Who's Lucy?"

"That's the name of her pet alien," Jimmy said.

"Oh," Jen replied. Then, her face grew serious. "Oh, no," she added, her voice shifting from slightly to definitely concerned.

"Oh, no?" I asked, noting the foreboding tone in her voice. "What do you mean, oh no?"

"Don't tell me your little sister was stupid enough to go looking for that thing?" asked Jen, placing her index finger on my chest.

"Travis, I hate to say it," Jimmy said, "but for someone with the highest I.Q. in the room, she's definitely the most stupid." He let out a pent up sigh and added, "Not to mention she's a royal pain in the ass too."

I nodded. The facts were the facts, and Jimmy wasn't wrong. "Let's put it this way," I replied to Jen's earlier question, "she's downright stubborn. Stubborn to the point of causing everyone grief."

"She's going to cause herself to get killed," Jen replied. "Hurry," she said, running over to the pile of our things and grabbing her swords. "We've got to get to her before they do."

"They? Who are they? What are you talking about?" asked Billy. "Save her from what? I thought we were on the safe side of the city."

"No," Jen replied, shaking her head. "We're on the not so safe side. It's just that I knew how to guide you safely to the Pendry. But, outside those walls," she said, pointing out the hotel window, "is alien territory. And your sister has walked right into the lion's den, so to speak."

"My sister can take care of herself."

"Don't be too sure of that, Travis. These creatures aren't like the tame one you brought with you. These are vicious killing machines. Every single one of them. And they'll tear your sister to shreds."

"I thought you said they don't ever bother you," Jimmy interrupted.

"They don't, because I keep to myself and don't encroach on their territory. But if she's just out their roaming free range, it's only a matter of time before one of the alien scouts finds her."

"Then we do what we always do," Billy said. "We band together and face our challenges head on."

"Renegades of Summer, on me," Sarah said, throwing out her hand.

We all huddled together, placing hands on hands in the center until all of us except for Jen had joined the team cheer. I looked over at Jen and then nodded at her to join the group.

She smiled and threw her hand onto the pile. Jimmy counted us down. "Three, two, one..."

"RENEGADES!" we cried out in unison.

3

REBELLION
PART 3: THE HIVE AND THE EGG

SIF CAUGHT SCENT OF MY SISTER IN A MATTER of minutes and took off up the street, running full bore. All we could do was follow after her, hoping she'd get to my sister ahead of us and help keep her safe.

With Sif on the case, Jen helped us navigate the nooks and crannies of the city without bumping into a single alien. In fact, it felt like a city wide game of hide and go seek, and we were winning. At least, that's what it seemed like until we turned the corner down by the pier at Hollywood Beach and found two massive aliens patrolling the area.

"Quick, take cover," Jen whispered.

Billy and I dove over the railing of the walkway that ran the length of the pier and dropped fifteen feet to the sand below. We hit the sand with a thud and rolled onto our backs, coughing and wheezing for air. Everyone else played it smart and ducked behind a nearby dumpster.

"What do you see," Billy asked, cupping his hands over his mouth to focus his whisper.

Sarah motioned her hand downward, as if to say hold, and we waited in anxious anticipation as one of the creatures came right up to the dumpsters. It sniffed the air, squawked, and scanned the area. Giving up, it squawked again and then turned back the way it had come, its six tails whipping through the air like agitated fire hoses.

"That was a close one," Billy said. He let out a sigh and then began to help Sarah down to our position.

I turned around and glanced under the pier and froze in my tracks. As Billy was helping Sarah, I reached over and tugged on his sleeve.

"Uh, guys..." I said. Billy finally got Sarah down and they helped Jimmy and Jen down after them. Megan hopped the railing and landed in a superhero styled pose on the sand. "Guys," I said, more intensely.

"What is it, Trav?" Sarah asked, noticing something was off with me.

When everyone turned to me, I merely raised my hand and pointed beneath the pier at the field of giant eggs that dappled the sand like a jewel encrusted crown.

"Holy cap!" Jimmy shouted.

Megan reached around and covered his mouth. "Shhh," she said, and with her other hand she pointed at the other side of the pier where the alien scouts from earlier had come down to beach level—probably to check on the eggs.

"Quick, over here," Jen called out, waving us over to the massive columns that supported the pier. "Keep to the shade and don't let those things see you."

Of course, we did as instructed and waited as the aliens inspected the eggs and then turned and resumed their patrol.

After they'd disappeared from sight, we gradually emerged from the shadows and Jimmy walked over to the closest row of eggs.

"What are you doing?" Billy asked.

"I've gotta see this for myself," Jimmy replied.

There was a palpable excitement in his voice.

Upon reaching the first row of eggs, Jimmy sank to his knees in the sand beside them and placed his hands on the nearest egg. The egg, which was slightly larger than a rugby ball and roughly the same shape, had a leathery, yet slimy texture. Jimmy didn't care though, and he put his ear to it.

Megan wiped some of the slime off an egg onto her fingers and then sniffed them. She raised an eyebrow and looked over at Sarah.

"What is it?" she asked.

"It smells nice. Kind of like freshly cut cucumbers, if you can believe it."

Billy followed her lead and did the same. "Oh, man. It really does smell like cucumbers."

"Guys," Jimmy said, bending down and placing his ear against the egg. "You've gotta hear this."

"Um, no thanks," Megan replied. "That's basically a snot-covered football. I'm fine right where I am." Megs folded her arms and took a step back.

Jen brushed past her, deliberately nudging her with her shoulder as she went on by. Megan rolled her eyes and turned her back to Jen who knelt down beside Billy and put her ear up against the same egg.

Their faces a hand's width apart, they both looked into each other's eyes with a sense of wonder and excitement. "You hear that?" Billy asked excitedly.

"Yes," Jen said, smiling at him.

Misreading the signs, Jimmy thought Jen's proximity maybe meant something and he leaned forward and kissed her on the lips. Drawing back when she didn't reciprocate the intimate act, Jimmy looked genuinely apologetic.

"I'm sorry, I thought we were sharing a moment and I—"

"You little shithead!" Jen screamed, shoving Jimmy away from her. He fell flat on his ass and looked up only to see her leap into the air. Drawing out a hidden knife from her back, she pounced on Jimmy, slammed him back onto the sand, and pressed the sharp edge of her blade against his throat. "Don't you ever touch me!"

"Hey, now," Billy said raising a cautious hand. "We're all allies here."

He took a step forward to try and diffuse the situation but Jen merely raised the blade and pointed it at him, her other hand around Jimmy's throat. "Not another step, player. Or your friend gets an eye wedged out."

"I didn't mean nothing by it," Jimmy wheezed through Jen's clamped fingers.

"Jennifer," I said. She didn't respond. "Jennifer," I repeated, more loudly this time. She finally looked over at me. "What, Travis?"

"He's my friend. And you're hurting him."

"This pimple-popping, zit-butt just kissed me. Maybe a good beating is what he deserves. Or maybe I just cut your lips off and call it even."

I couldn't explain it even if I wanted to, but Jen's eyes were wild, but scared all at the same time. Jimmy accidentally triggered a trauma response and she'd turned into the stone-cold killer that Lucy had shown me in the vision. Or, more likely, had warned me of.

"Babe," I said, stepping aside. With a simple wave of the hand, I gestured for her to proceed. "If you'd be so kind as to save Jimmy."

"Oh, baby," Megan said excitedly, hopping up and down as she cracked her neck from side to side. Rolling her shoulders and balling up her fists, she added, "It would be my absolute pleasure."

Dashing forward like a raging bull, Megan tackled Jen and they tumbled through the sand, rolling twice and kicking up a spray of dirt.

"Get off of me," Jen shouted.

"Don't hurt our resident pervert, you psycho!" was Megans reply as she sprang up just as Jen started to push herself up off the ground.

Before Jen could get to her feet, Megan grabbed her by the hair and need her right in her face. There was a resounding crunch and Megan's nose began gushing blood. Touching her face, she looked down at her fingers to see them soaked in crimson. "You bitch!" Jen screamed. "You broke my nose."

"That's just bone one of two hundred and six, you backbiting, boyfriend stealing, trollop!"

With lightning speed, Jen threw her knife at Megan and it embedded itself between Megan's shoulder and upper pectoral region. But like the freaking Terminator, Megan grabbed the knife, tore it out, and threw it into the sand beside her feet.

A large if not entirely alarming smile formed on Meg's face signaling she was just getting started. Without intending it, Jen had awakened the She-Hulk. And Megan was berserking hardcore.

"Oh, crap," Jen said, realizing she was going to get pummeled into a bloody stump.

Not wasting another second on this cat-fight, she turned to run away, but Billy, being Billy, stepped back making sure to leave one leg extended so that Jen ran past she would trip. Sure enough, just as planned, her foot snagged on Billy's foot and she tumbled to the ground.

Face planting into the dirt, Jen pushed herself back up and spat out globs of sand. "Blek. Disgusting."

Megan dashed past us and tackled Jen around the waist and dragged her back down to the ground again. If roller derby and competitive shooting weren't enough, Megs also had about six years of Judo training and was currently a first degree black belt.

As they tussled about, Megs pulled off Jen's pink sweats, exposing her powerful thighs and black underwear. Kicking to get away from Megan, who clawed at her like a ferocious jungle Panther, Jen abandoned her sweats and stood up, beach sand sticking to her butt and thighs.

"Hey, Jen… what's the matter?" asked Megan.

"Are you done dancing so soon? Because my punch card is wide open and I'm ready to tango."

Jen's eyes constantly scanned us as she slowly backed away. Her eyes wild with fright, she held out a finger and pointed it at all of us. "You people really are crazy! Like, literally *Coocoo's Nest,* padded walls level of insane. I knew I should have never taken you in."

"Crazy? Us?" Jimmy asked, rising to his feet. "Look who's talking, you super sexy fruitcake."

Jen shook a finger at him and groaned angrily. It was as if she wanted to admonish him some more but couldn't think of anything to say so she choked down a groan.

"Jennifer," Sarah said, raising her hand and cautiously walking toward her. "I was there, remember? I was there when that alien killed Dean, Mike, Tina, Abby, Tim, and... Ryan. Remember? I'm in this with you."

She lingered on Ryan's name, because that was Jen's boyfriend and, sadly, one of the casualties of the Massacre at Make-Out Point.

Jen's arms fell limp by her sides and she began sobbing, large heavy sobs. "Why did they have to die? Why?"

"I don't know," Sarah replied as she slowly wrapped her arms around Jen and gave her a warm embrace. "I don't know. All I know is, we're here. You and me. And, like it or not, we are the only ones who can carry on their memory. And I intend to do just that."

Still sobbing, Jen buried her face into Sarah's shoulder. "It's not fair," she said. "It's just not fair."

"I know, sweetie," Sarah replied, tenderly stroking Jen's back. "But life isn't ever fair. And we can never predict when it will be our time. All we can do is try our best to be descent to one another during the time we have."

Megan looked over at me and then Jimmy and, taking a deep breath, finally found her calm. No longer combative, Megs came over and stood by me. Touching her arm, she winced from a twinge of pain caused by her fresh knife wound.

"We'll have to get that cleaned and patched up, as soon as possible," I said.

Megan nodded, looked over at me, and smiled. "Thanks Travis," she said. She let her fingers gently brush my fingers as our hands flirted by our sides.

"For what?" I asked.

"For letting me get that out of my system."

"Oh, well, she sort of had it coming."

"I don't know," Jimmy said. "All things considered, I found it kind of hot."

"Of course you did," Megan said. "You're our resident pervert. If you didn't get turned on by a strong woman jumping onto you and holding a blade to your throat, then we'd all be really worried about you. Like, properly worried."

We all had a good laugh. Even Jen fought through her sniffles and laughed along with us. All the same, being the butt of the joke aside, she recognized she was the one in the wrong, and after taking a moment to calm down, Jen walked up to Jimmy and apologized.

"I'm sorry. It wasn't my intent to hurt you, I just... I don't know. I guess I have a lot of unprocessed trauma given everything that's happened to me in the past couple of weeks. I shouldn't have taken it out on you. I hope you're not too hurt by my bull crap."

"Only my pride," Jimmy said. "I mean, after last night and everything, I really thought maybe you liked me or something."

"Last night?" asked Jen, stepping back and cocking her head. "What I do last night?"

"You don't remember?" Jimmy asked.

"You took your top off and hugged him," Billy said, having Jimmy's back.

"I did?"

We all nodded.

"Now I really do feel like the biggest fool on the planet."

"You might say that" Jimmy teased.

Jen let a reserved laugh slip out, but it was filled with embarrassment and perhaps a little self-loathing.

Staring up at the bottom of the pier, Jen let out a long exasperated sigh. "I guess I can see why you thought I was coming onto you. I'm really good at sending mixed signals. Again, I'm sorry for all my idiotic behavior."

"Apology accepted," Jimmy said as he bent down and gathered up her pink sweatpants and handed them to her.

"Thanks," she said, accepting his generosity and the wadded up bundle of sandy sweatpants.

"I hate to break up this wonderful Kumbaya moment," Billy Bardem interjected, "But we have some spectators."

We all turned around to find the two aliens from earlier standing no more than fifty meters away, watching us and looking at the eggs and then at us. Since our skirmish had caused us to move away from the eggs, they were trying to assess if we were an imminent threat or not.

Once they realized that we weren't that big of a threat, they began to slowly move toward us perchance to herd us away from their young.

"Everyone… run!" Jen shouted, spinning around and grabbing Jimmy's hand as she turned to flee. "Move your asses… now!"

We all took off, sprinting down Hollywood Beach, Lake Michigan on our right, the sprawling city on our left.

Running through the soft sand was one of the hardest things we'd ever attempted. If my sister would have been here, someone would have had to carry her. After all, Renegades of summer never left one of their own behind.

So, when Jen stopped mid stride and let go of

Jimmy's hand, we all glanced back to see what was happening.

Jen threw her pink sweatpants onto the beach and then turned back toward us. As she ran, putting as much distance between herself and the Hunter Killer aliens as she could, the creatures stopped at the sweatpants and began sniffing and clawing at them. Each alien grabbed one pant leg, starting a vicious game of tug of war. With snarls and snorts, they ripped the sweats in half.

Jen pointed at the stairs that led to the street and said, "You guys ditch them in the city. We'll meet up again at the hospital. Look for the guarded gate on the north facing side. Go, find your mom."

As we turned up the stairs to streetside, Jen shot past us and kept running up the beach. Jimmy blew past us too and continued up the beach, following Jen. "What are you doing?"

"I'm buying you time," she said as Jimmy jogged alongside her. "They have my scent. They'll stay on me."

"I think you mean… on us," Jimmy said. He then looked over his shoulder at us and smiled, giving us a small salute as his way of saying goodbye, and then spun back around and ran with Jen up the beach.

"Jimmy!" I shouted, reaching out my hand.

Megan grabbed me, and shook her head. "He's made up his mind, Trav. We've gotta go."

Billy helped usher Sarah, Megan, and me up the stairs and looked back one last time. Sure enough, the aliens ignored us and kept on running after Jen and Jimbo.

"Good luck, Mad Dog," Billy said. With that, he raced up the steps and we turned down Forty-first Street onto Lakeshore Drive.

None of us knew whether running out in the open streets like this was a good idea, but since Jen had successfully diverted the scouts, we were willing to risk being out in the open. Especially considering the fact that it was a straight shot to the hospital.

The walk took us roughly two and a half hours, but we finally saw the guarded gate that Jen had told us about.

Having a bunch of kids stroll up was probably the last thing they were expecting, but Billy and Sarah took point. Roughly a quarter mile away, they waved at the guards and drew their attention to us. A couple of Marines ran up to us, meeting us halfway.

"What are you kids doing out in the open like this? It's not safe out here."

"We came from Woodridge," I said. "We're looking for my mom, Emily Mahoney. She's a nurse. We were told she was evacuated from Woodridge General to Northwest Memorial, here in Chicago."

"I don't know whether there's an Emily Mahoney on staff or not. But you kids better come with us and get off these streets."

The Marines escorted us to the front gates, past some concrete road dividers and two brand new Humvees, which were basically Jeep Wranglers on steroids. Both Humvees had fifty-cal gun turrets mounted on them. If that wasn't rad enough, there was a single M1 Abrams tank with 120 millimeter cannon wedged between them.

"That's a lot of firepower," I whispered. Billy nodded.

"No wonder the aliens haven't been able to breach this section of the city."

"Nobody does overkill like the U.S. military," Sarah added.

Megan reached up and ran her fingers along the canon barrel of the tank. "It just emanates raw, masculine energy. Is it weird that I'm a little turned on right now?"

"Oh, you behave," Sarah said, laughing at Megan's joke.

"Please don't touch the ordnance," the Marine said, looking back at Megan.

"Sorry," she giggled. She then looked over at me, her eyes wide with surprise.

All I could do was laugh in return, because her eyes seemed to keep on getting bigger and bigger as she stared at me with a salacious grin on her face. It was the type of grin you'd expect to see on a girl's face if she had unexpectedly walked in on the high school wrestling team changing in the locker room, and was amused rather than mortified by it.

Soon enough, we passed a tent with several officers chatting on the com-station, two more Marine centurions standing in front of sandbags stacked knee-high and which lined the entrance in a staggered "V" pattern. I could only assume that it was probably for use as additional cover in case of a breach. If the aliens breached, several Marines could take up positions behind the sand bags and maybe avoid getting lashed to death by those glowing tail-whips.

Finally, we came to an inner chain-link fence just behind the main walls, adding a second heavily guarded checkpoint that we needed to pass through before entering the closed-off section of the city.

Two additional Marines and a third Humvee with a Marine poking out of the cupula hatch manned the fifty-cal acted as the final safeguard before being allowed into the city. I happened to notice that the chain-link fence was also electrified and I nodded at Billy who nodded back, signaling that he noticed it too.

"If you kids have any weapons on you, leave them here, at the gate." The nearest Marine pointed to a fold out table nearby and we nodded.

"Yes, sir," Billy replied, as he set his shotgun onto the table. We all followed suit, stripping off our blades and gear and setting it onto the table.

A second Marine came over and had us fan our arms and legs as he ran a metal detector wand over us, just to make sure. Once we were cleared, he hit a red button on a silver mounted control box and the metal gate slid open, allowing us access to the inner sanctum.

"Welcome to Chicago, kids," the guard said, and gestured for us to head on inside.

As we passed through the opening, we looked up at the twenty foot concrete walls as we entered what would only be described as a four block wide thriving village.

The remaining population of Chicago seemed to consist primarily of vital personnel only, seeing as there were no children or elderly people out and about. There were scientists, soldiers, construction crews, and food delivery people. There was the smell of food, the sounds of people chatting, and even cars honking as they weaved about the flood of pedestrians.

An army-green painted jeep pulled up alongside of us and a woman soldier looked at all of our faces and then said, "I got a call that a bunch of kids roamed in from the wild." She looked at us again, "You best hop in and I'll take you to Memorial to get you all checked out. As soon as you finish your medical checks, you'll be allowed back into general populace."

"We're looking for my mom," I said. "She's a nurse."

"It's a good thing we're headed that way, then." She smiled at me and I held out my hand.

"My name is Travis Mahoney. And you are?"

She took my hand, shook it, and replied, "I'm Sergeant First Class, Naomi Renteria Rodriguez." Then, jutting a thumb at the back seat, she said, "Pile in."

Sarah climbed in the back and said, "Thank you so much, we've been walking all day."

"Yeah, thanks," Billy said.

I squeezed into the back seat between Billy and Sarah while Megan took the front passenger seat next to Sergeant Rodriguez. When she plopped down in the seat, the entire jeep rocked and Sergeant Rodriguez looked over at Megan and raised an eyebrow.

"Wow, you're a sturdy girl, aren't you? Have you ever thought about a career in the Military?"

Megan smiled. "It's sounding more and more like a possibility, Sergeant."

Sergeant Naomi Rodriguez smiled, then turned the key in the ignition and the jeep roared to life.

"Hold on to your seats," the Sergeant said, as she hit the clutch and shifted it into first. The jeep lurched forward and we were off.

Sergeant Naomi Rodriguez weaved in and out of bustling traffic and pedestrians, never honking her horn and rarely tapping the breaks. It seemed as though this was a drive she'd made daily and knew the ins and outs of the city like the back of her hand.

Five short minutes later, we arrived at the front entrance of Northwestern Memorial Hospital.

The jeep's breaks screeched in protest as we skidded to an abrupt stop. "See you kids later," the sergeant said. Then, turning to Megan, she added, "And I hope to see you in a year or two, fighting by my side."

"I look forward to it," Megan replied, and she gave the sergeant an informal salute.

Naomi merely nodded and then shifted the jeep into gear as we hopped out. Nearly the moment we'd exited her vehicle, Sergeant Rodriguez tore away, doing a quick U-turn that squealed the tires as she headed back the way we'd come.

"What took you dipsticks so long?" asked a small yet familiar voice.

All of us spun around to find my sister, Melody, sitting on a bench, safe and sound, eating a ham and cheese sandwich.

"Melody!" Sarah shouted, elated and relieved all at the same time. Sarah raced over to Melody, scooped her up in her arms, and swung her in several circles before setting her back down. "We were so worried about you."

"I'm fine," Melody said.

"Hey, stink-breath," I said.

Melody looked over at me and smiled. "Hey, fart-face."

I opened my arms wide, and Melody ran toward me. I braced myself for the impact but when she ran past me, I turned to watch as she flung herself into the arms of Billy Bardem.

"I missed you sooo much, Billy."

"It's been less than eight hours," I said under my breath, unable to mask the sarcasm.

"I missed you too, kid," Billy replied. He then bent down and kissed Melody on the head, his hands resting on her shoulders. "I'm glad you're safe."

Billy then turned and entered the hospital.

"Did that just happen?" Melody asked. "Did Billy Bardem just kiss me?"

"You're leveling up, I see," Megan said, winking

at Mel as she passed.

"I think I might have some competition," Sarah added, hooking her elbow around Mel's and linking arms. She and Melody shared a laughed and then they followed everyone else into the hospital.

I was also about to head in when I unexpectedly heard a bark. Pausing, I turned to see Sif trotting toward me. "Woof! Woof!"

"Hey, girl!" I said, dropping to my knees to give Sif all the scritch-and-scratches she could ever want. "I'm so glad to see you. I guess you found Melody and kept her safe." I pulled Sif in and hugged the furry golden lab and let her lick my face.

As I was petting Sif, someone called out my name. "Travis?"

Looking up, I saw my mother standing over me and tears immediately burst from my eyes. "Mom!"

She raced up to me and, sinking to her knees, threw her arms around me and held me tight. I couldn't help it, but I broke down sobbing in my mother's embrace.

"Don't worry, Travis," she whispered as she held me by the back of my neck, her other hand stroking my back. "You're safe now."

4

REBELLION
PART 4: OASIS AMIDST CHAOS

"THE LAST STARFIGHTER? YOU'RE INSANE IF you think *The Last Starfighter* trumps *Tron*. *Tron* is the defining science fiction film of our generation!"

"Don't be a dweeb. I didn't say *The Last Starfighter* was the defining science fiction film of our generation. That win clearly goes to Ridley Scott's horror sci-fi masterpiece *Alien*. All I'm saying is that *The Last Starfighter* is inherently a better film than *Tron*. It even has better computer graphics."

"Aight. I agree with you that *Alien* is the defining sci-fi film in all of history. Better than Kubrik's *2001* and better than *Flash Gordon*. But, is it better than *The Wrath of Khan?*"

"Star Trek? Get wrecked, bro. Star Wars is a million times superior to cowboys in space."

"You're wrong. Star Trek is sophisticated. Star

Wars is just space fantasy hokum with laser swords."

"Heh-hem," I said loudly, clearing my throat as Mitch and Paul sat in the waiting room of the fifth floor medical wing arguing about their favorite science fiction movies. "Are you both idiots or what? Because James Cameron's *Aliens* is a thousand times better than *Alien*. As for Star Trek and Star Wars, well, they're opposite sides of the same space-fantasy coin. Besides, everyone knows that *Maximum Overdrive* is the greatest science fiction film ever made."

"Maximum Overdrive?" Paul and Mitch balked at the same time turning to face the moron who dared suggest such an absurd thing. As one of the worst Stephen King produced B-films of all time, *Maximum Overdrive* was a dumpster fire of a film that was so bad that it had to be seen in order to be believed.

When they saw Sarah, Billy, Megan, Melody, and me standing on the opposite side of the room, their faces lit up.

"Travis?" Paul gasped. "Billy? Sarah?!"

"Yep," I said, gesturing at the rest of the gang. "We're all here."

Unable to hold back our emotions, we all burst

into laughter and hugged and embraced one another. After the excitement died down, Paul drew back, looked right at me, and said, "You'd better be kidding about that *Maximum Overdrive* comment."

I laughed. "Of course I am. That movie is a piece of crap. I just had to get your guys' attention since you were too engrossed in your conversation to even notice that we'd entered the room."

"Oh, yeah, sorry about that," Mitch said. "I guess we got carried away."

"Besides," Megan chimed in. "Everyone knows that the movie *Wraith*, starring Charlie Sheen, is the best science fiction film of the century."

"Of the century?" balked Mitch. "You're only saying that because you think he's hot!"

"Fair enough," Megan said, laughing. Mitch smiled and they hugged.

"Come here, you little goober," Megan said, giving her brother a bearhug and a noogie to ruffle up his hair.

"What are you guys doing here?" asked Billy.

"Yeah, last we heard you had chosen to stay back in Woodridge. So, what gives?" asked Sarah.

"The town is gone, man," Paul informed us.

"Like, blasted off the face of the map gone."

"Yeah, yeah," Mitch added. "Not even twenty-four hours after you guys left, the military rolled in with a full contingency of troops and went to war with about fifty of those aliens."

"My dad evacuated the church and we all piled onto the old school bus the church bought for mission trips and drove here, to Chicago."

I looked at Paul. "Where's your dad now?"

"With my mom," Paul replied. "Why?"

"No, dickhole," Melody said, speaking up. "He meant, where are they? Are they alive? Did they rapture up to heaven? Or decided to just orphan their kids by leaving them in some random hospital waiting room?"

"Language, young lady!" my mom's voice rang out. Suddenly a hand reached between Billy and me, and grabbed ahold of my sister's ear. "Am I going to have to wash your mouth out with soap, young lady?"

"Ow, ow… Mom! You're hurting me."

"You'll live," my mom replied, finally letting go of Melody's ear. Then, pointing a finger at her, she said, "I don't want to hear that kind of language again. Do I make myself clear?”

“Yes, ma’am,” Melody said, casting her eyes down at her feet.

“Good. Now, the rest of you, get something to eat. There are sandwiches and chips in the breakroom down the hall. Help yourself to as many as you want. I’ll swing by and check on you all in an hour or so, but my shift starts...” she looked down at her wrist and checked her watch and, frowning, said, “Seven minutes ago.”

My mom gave me another hug, ruffled Melody’s hair, and then raced off to start her shift.

Mitch finally answered Billy’s earlier question on behalf of Paul, who’d already forgotten about it. “To answer Billy’s question though,” Mitch said, “Paul’s dad is in the hospital chapel as a volunteer trauma caregiver. His mom is helping with check-ins and check-outs here at the hospital.”

“What about mom and dad?” asked Megan.

“Oh, they’re in Michigan, at Grandma and Grandpa’s,” Mitch said. “They left a note. They should be fine.” Mitch reached into his back pocket and pulled out a folded piece of lined yellow legal paper and handed it to Megan.

Megan carefully unfolded the note and silently read it to herself. I could see a huge weight was lifted from Megan's shoulders as she let out a lengthy sigh and reached down and took my hand and squeezed. "Thank God," she said, handing the note back to Mitch who took it and stuffed it back into his pocket again.

Paul looked around the group and then asked, "Where's Jimmy? I thought he was with you guys."

"About that..." I said, pausing to try and figure out how best to broach the subject.

"He's basically following the advice of his nob-goblin instead of using common sense to realize he's placed himself in mortal danger to try and win the affection of a girl who, earlier today, tried to slit his throat," Megan informed them.

"Wait," Mitch said, shooting her a curious look. "What girl?"

"Jennifer Nakamura," Sarah said, answering Mitch's question.

"The smoking hot Asian chick?" he asked.

"She's not that hot," Megan said, folding her arms and pouting.

"Actually," Paul said, pushing up his glasses as he

exuded an air of sophistication, "She was ranked number one among the Fort Liberty Renegades as being the most likely to graduate and become a super model."

"It's just Renegades now," I informed him.

He nodded. "That makes sense, considering Fort Liberty is just a memory at this point."

"Super model, my ass," Megan retorted.

"Why are you such a sour-puss today?" asked Mitch.

"Oh, Megs and Jen got into it today," I informed them. "They quite literally tried to kill each other."

"Yeah," Billy said. "Your sister was defending the honor of Jimmy, who Jen had at knife point."

"You defended Jimmy 'Mad Dog' Polson?" Mitch's jaw fell slack and he stared at his sister. "What has gotten into you?"

"I have no idea," she said. "I guess I must be mentally ill, or something."

"So, what the heck happened after that?" asked Paul, engrossed by our wild adventures.

"Now, Jen and Jimmy are on the run. They used themselves as bait to draw two Hunter Killers away from us and give us a chance to escape," Sarah said.

"Right now, we don't know where they are or if they're safe. All we can do is keep our fingers crossed," added Billy.

At that moment, an alarm went off and nurses and doctors began rushing around.

"What's going on?" I asked.

Paul and Mitch looked unphased, but then Paul said, "Oh, that's just the emergency alarm for incoming. Usually it's a bunch of soldiers that got scraped up fighting the aliens. Every now and then it's a bystander who was in the wrong place at the wrong time."

"It's not a big deal," Mitch said. "It happens twenty times a day."

"Right now," Paul said, "Your mom told us to take you all to the breakroom to get something to eat. And I'm starving."

"You're always starving," Billy said, slapping Paul on the back and walking with him toward the breakroom.

"You guys go on ahead," I said, hanging back and looking down the long medical corridor.

"What is it?" asked Megan.

"I don't know. Maybe it's just the timing. Maybe

it's nothing. But I have a bad feeling about this."

"Do you want me to come with you?"

"No," I said, looking at her beautiful baby-blue eyes. "I'll just check it out and come right back to join you all for lunch. Go get something to eat."

She smiled, gave me a quick hug, and jogged to catch up to the others.

I went down to the E.R. and snuck in behind the mad-dash of nurses. Either nobody noticed me or they were too busy to care, but I found a cart being wheeled in. On the gurney, was a badly bloodied and beaten Jimmy. Straddling him, was Jen, who was frantically administering CPR as two medics wheeled them in.

Jen was giving Jimmy mouth to mouth, and I couldn't help but notice that she still had on her black panties, her blood-stained white tank top, and nothing else. Whatever had happened to them, it wasn't good.

A doctor stopped the cart and a nurse grabbed Jen's forearm. "We'll take it from here, hon."

Another nurse helped Jen off the gurney and they put a breathing apparatus on Jimmy's face and started pumping air into him as they wheeled him away.

"Don't die on me, you little perv. Do you hear me? Don't you dare die!"

The nurses wheeled Jimmy away and Jen stood, obviously in shock, and watched him disappear behind some swinging doors as they took him into the O.R. to try and save his life.

"Jen?" I said, realizing she hadn't noticed me standing behind her.

Jen turned around and when she saw it was me, she broke down crying and ran up to me and threw her arms around me.

I let her get it all out and held her until she stopped trembling. After a long wait, I finally asked her, "What happened?"

"The idiot jumped in front of me to save me from a barbed tail to my heart. That should have been me on that cart. Not him."

She broke down again and I hugged her tight.

"Miss," a nurse said, gently touching Jen's arm. "If you'd like to come with me, we'll get you stitched up."

"I'm fine," Jen said.

"No you're not," I said, grabbing her by the

shoulders and forcing her to look me in the eyes. "You're cut and your bleeding."

Jen looked down at her thighs and found five lacerations. Three more on her arms. One on her neck. "Oh," she said, realizing, for the first time, how badly wounded she truly was. Looking back up at me, she blinked. Her face was calm and collected, but I could sense fear in her eyes. "Will you come with me, keep me company?"

"Of course," I said.

The nurse guided us to a room and I looked down to find Jen was holding my hand. She held my hand through the whole ordeal, not letting go for an instant.

Once the nurse had stitched and bandaged her up, she asked if she could get Jen a fresh set of clothes. Jen nodded.

"Are you okay?" I asked.

The moment the nurse left the patient room to get Jen some fresh clothes, Jen's fingers touched my face and drew me into her. Her lips crashed into mine and she kissed me long and good. It was the sultriest kiss I'd ever had.

I drew back and stammered, "I, uh, I have, um, a

Megan. I mean, Megan and I, we, uh, are dating. So, I… um…"

"I know that," Jen answered, feeling embarrassed. She buried her face into her palms and chastised herself. "Stupid, stupid, stupid."

I grabbed her wrist and pulled her hands away from her face. "No, you're not stupid. You're hurting. And I'm here to give you any support I can. Including kissing you, if that makes you feel better."

I instantly kicked myself for saying something so idiotic. What was I, the Pity Party Brigade? Jen was a big girl. She didn't need a Knight in Shining Armor to rescue her. She certainly didn't need a boyfriend.

"I see why Megan likes you. You're genuinely sweet. And you're probably the sincerest person I've ever met, Travis. But I'm afraid if I kiss you again, I won't stop. So, you know. Maybe we just forget it ever happened."

"You sure?"

Jen laughed. "I mean, do you want to cheat on Megan?"

"Oh, Hell no," I said. "She'd kill me."

"See? So, maybe we just stay friends?" She held out her hand, offering a handshake. But when I went to take her hand I accidently rammed my hand straight into her left boob.

"Oh, crap. I mean… I'm sorry. I wasn't trying to…"

"It's all right, Trav," Jen laughed. "It was an accident."

"Uh, yeah," I said nervously rubbing the back of my neck. "Totally an accident."

Jen looked over to find Megan standing in the doorway watching us. "Hey, Megs," Jen said, sliding off the medical table. "You've got a keeper here."

With that said, Jen walked past Megan who stepped aside and watched her walk back through the emergency room doors and straight out of the hospital.

"What was that about?"

"It's Jimmy," I said.

Megs turned back toward me. "Please tell me he's not…"

"No," I said. "He's still alive. But he's in a bad way. They have him in the O.R. right now."

"That's terrible."

I nodded. "If it wasn't for Jen, he'd be dead."

Megs looked back again. I could tell she was

thinking what I was thinking. Even though her and Jen butted heads from time to time, at the end of the day, Jen was one of us. Jen was a true Renegade. And she didn't deserve to be left alone to wallow in her failures or her self-doubt.

"Hold on," Megan said, sprinting out of the hospital after Jennifer Nakamura.

A couple minutes later the nurse returned with Jen's clothes, but since I was the only one still in the patient room, she handed them to me and disappeared on urgent business again.

Megs returned with her arm draped around Jen's shoulders, fresh tears in Jen's eyes.

"Here," I said, handing Jen the pile of neatly folded clothes. "The nurse gave these to me to give you."

Jen took the clothes without looking at them and smiled at me. "You truly are the sweetest guy ever," she said. Then, she leaned forward and kissed me on the cheek.

"He really is," Megs said, and she too leaned over and kissed me on my other cheek.

"On that we can agree," Jen said, and she kissed me on my right cheek again.

"Definitely," Megan answered, and kissed my left cheek.

Whatever this was had suddenly turned into a competition between them, and Megs and Jen were kissing both of my cheeks in rapid succession to see who could get the most kisses in the least amount of time.

"Travis, what's going on here?"

We all looked over to find my mom standing in near us, arms folded across her chest as she shot us a discerning gaze.

"Oh, hi Mrs. Mahoney!" Megan said. "Travis and I are dating now."

"Ohhh," Jen said, as she pieced together that it was my mom staring at her. "Travis is your boy?"

"Yes," my mom replied. "He's my baby boy. And you two fine young ladies seem to be accosting him."

I laughed. "They're not accosting me, mom. Not much, anyway."

"Uh-huh," my mom replied, sounding rather unconvinced. "Well, this is the E.R., so if you don't mind taking yourself elsewhere to continue, well, whatever this is… I'd much appreciate it."

"Right, mom. Sorry."

"Yeah, sorry Mrs. Mahoney," Megan said.

"Mrs. Mahoney," Jen said, "I think you raised this kid right. He's the best guy I know. And, the moment Megan drops the ball, I'm snatching him right up."

"Like Hell you are!" Megan said, grabbing my hand and towing me toward the main lobby. "He's mine… forever."

"Forever?" I asked.

"Hey," Jen said, trailing after us. "Wait for me!"

My mom watched us leave, and hollered after us. "And put some clothes on, young lady!"

Jen merely swiveled around, waved to my mom, and disappeared with us behind the swinging doors as we entered the main lobby.

With Megan on my left arm and Jen on my right, we walked through the hospital lobby, all eyes on us. Everything seemed to be in slow motion, and as we past a reflective column in the middle of the room, I realized how dumb my big ole smile looked.

What's more, I also noticed the numerous lipstick stains of the two toned kiss marks that dappled my cheeks. Which would explain why I was getting so many weird looks from the patients and staff.

Once we returned to the fifth floor, Jen put on her new clothes, which were some tight fitting jeans and a burgundy t-shirt with sharp V-neck crop-top that teased hear cleavage and abdomen.

"So, how bad is it?" asked Sarah, piecing the events together based on the fact that Jen had returned with us but Jimmy hadn't.

Taking a deep breath, I composed myself and said, "He's alive. But barely."

"My second question is this," Sarah turned to me at the same time that Paul, Mitch, Billy, and my sister did, which was a little unnerving to say the least. "Why do you have a dozen different colored kiss-marks on both sides of your face?"

"Oh… that," I said, a sheepish grin forming on my face. "It's a long story."

"We were just trying to embarrass him in front of his mom," Megan informed the group.

Megan and Jen then shared a look and, realizing how silly they were being, burst into a fit of laughter and fell into one another's arms. They were barely able to stand they were laughing so hard.

"Well, this is a nice change of pace," Billy said,

looking over at them.

"At least they're not trying to kill each other anymore," Sarah agreed. "That's progress."

Megan got me a couple ham and cheese sandwiches and a bag of Lay's potato chips. I ate while Jen used a rag and some olive oil to wipe away the stains of my cheeks.

"So, how long had this been going on?" Melody looked over at me, Jen, and Megan, scanning all of our faces with an intense probing look as she noisily chewed her food. Not even waiting for my answer, she added, "What are you, some kind of pimp?"

"And where on Earth did you learn that word, young lady?" my mom's voice asked.

Melody's eyes grew impossibly large and she gulped down her last bite of food as she stared right at me. "She's standing behind me, isn't she?"

I nodded and looked up at my mom who, as Melody had correctly guessed, was standing directly behind her, arms folded, a scowl settling across her overly stern face.

Melody slowly swiveled around in her chair and chuckled nervously, batting her big brown eyes at our mother. "Oh, hi mom. What's up?"

"My foot will be up that rear derriere of yours in a second, young lady, if you don't start to speak with a little more respect." My mom was practically shaking, but I knew she was holding back her temper, trying not to blow up in front of everyone.

"Mom," I said, stepping between her and my sister. "It's okay."

"No, it's not okay, Travis," she began, tears already welling up around her eyes. "Your sister sounds like a foul-mouthed sailor fresh on shore leave." Fresh tears trickled out of the corners of her eyes and she broke down, the stress of the past week and a half finally getting to her.

I immediately hugged her and my sister did too. Then, Sarah, Billy, and Megan put their hands on my mom's body as she had herself a brief cry.

"I'm sorry," she apologized. "I'm supposed to be the adult here."

"Emily," Sarah said, addressing my mom directly. "You've had nothing but nonstop stress and worry for nearly two weeks not knowing whether your children were dead or alive. Plus you've been here at the hospital dealing with death, carnage, and a steady stream of trauma patients since the meteor shower decimated half the city. We just want you to know, we're here now. And we're not going anywhere."

As we joined my mom in a massive group hug, a doctor wearing a long, white medical coat entered the breakroom from the side entrance, walked over to the coffee machine, and began to poor himself a fresh pot of coffee.

When I looked up, I saw Sarah Lewis standing across from me petrified, her entire body trembling, her terrified eyes fixed on the stranger who'd entered the room moments ago. When I looked over to see what it was that had her so rattled, I saw the man we hoped we'd never see again.

Leaning against the counter, holding a mug of freshly brewed coffee in his hand, he smiled at us with an unnerving grin that betrayed his sinister intentions.

"Dr. Castle," I said, my tone as sharp and biting as broken glass.

Everyone's heads snapped up and all eyes locked onto Dr. Castle and we instinctively huddled around Sarah to give her added protection. Jen looked at us and then turned her gaze toward the doctor and then my mom, who appeared to be equally confused.

"What's going on, now?" asked my mom.

There was no time to fill her in on the fact that this plain old villain had deliberately poisoned Sarah, experimented on all of us as though we were lab rats, and had murdered all forty of his colleagues. I couldn't tell her that if we hadn't escaped his house of bloody horrors when we did, we'd all be dead right now.

In that moment, I knew I had to warn her of the sheer amount of danger we were all in and how dire our situation truly was. So, I said the only thing I could think of to say that would get the message across.

Reaching over, I took my mom's hand in mine and squeezed to get her attention. As our eyes met, I said, "Code Silver."

5

REBELLION
PART 5: DR. CASTLE RETURNS

Fight, run, hide. That was the Code Silver protocol as I understood it. Although it typically referred to an active shooter, it had the broader sense of describing a situation so dangerous that the only thing you could do was fight, run, or hide. And, by the look on my mom's face, she understood.

"Dr. Castle," my mom said, smiling at him. As she addressed him, she squeezed my hand back to let me know that she'd received my message loud and clear. "I don't believe you've had the pleasure to meet my kids."

"No, I would have remembered if I had," Dr. Castle lied.

My mom turned toward me, placed a hand on my shoulder, and then reached over and touched

Melody's head. "This is my son, Travis, and my daughter, Melody," she informed him. Then she looked at the rest of the gang, and said, "And these are their classmates and friends from school."

"Well, it's a pleasure to meet all of you," Dr. Castle said, raising his mug as he gestured a friendly salutations. Then he took a long sip of his coffee, his eyes watching us the entire time.

After his unusually long sip, he looked down at his watch and said, "Well, my break time is up." Before exiting the break room, however, he paused and looked right at me. "It was nice meeting you, Travis. Your mom is one of the best nurses we have on staff."

With that, he disappeared out of the room and Sarah, who'd been holding her breath nearly the whole time, took in a huge gasp of air.

"Who was that?" Paul asked.

"Yeah," Mitch demanded to know, "Why did you all tense up when that guy entered the room."

"He's bad news," Melody said.

"He tried to murder Sarah," Billy said, locking eyes with Sarah Lewis.

"Dr. Castle," Jen said, tapping her chin as she

thought. "Why does that name sound so familiar?"

"He's from the CDC," my mom correctly relayed. "He's one of our main lab techs. He showed up about three days ago. But as far as I know he's been doing an exceptional job."

"That will change," I said.

"Dr. Castle," Jen murmured to herself. She was still thinking on it when, suddenly, her eyes lit up and she snapped her fingers. "Oh, now I remember."

"What?" asked Sarah.

"When I was tracking you guys, I came across an abandoned parking lot with dozens of dead bodies. They were all so pale, like zombies."

"Zombies?" asked Paul.

"Not real zombies," I said. "He just poisons people with this cocktail drug he invented."

"What's the drug do?" asked Mitch. "I mean, what's it supposed to do?"

"Supposedly," Megan replied, "it's supposed to be a vaccine against the aliens—who he thinks are rewriting our DNA to turn us into them."

"But that's not how DNA works," my mom said.

"I know. It's all pseudoscience and quackery," I said. "But he believes everyone is infected and is on a mission to cleanse the planet."

"If everything you say is accurate," my mom interjected, then I'll have to report this. You kids wait here while I go find the Chief of Medicine and have a little chat about our mutual acquaintance, Dr. Castle."

My mom exited the room and we all looked at one another. This was the first time in several weeks that we didn't know what to do with ourselves.

"I don't know about you, guys," Jen said, "but I'm going to head back to the hotel."

"Hotel?" Paul asked, scanning our faces for any details that would help him understand what it was we were talking about.

"Yeah. Jen's parents rented a suite at the Pendry. But they were evacuated, so she's been staying there, waiting for them to contact her."

"It's not outside of the wall, is it?" Mitch gulped nervously. "Because things out there are not going great."

"The military can barely keep the aliens at bay. Right now, we're cloistered off from the rest of the city and the aliens are content to let us have this small section of town. But they've taken over everything else.," Paul informed us.

"Most people who leave the confines of the wall don't come back," Mitch said. "We've only been here a few days, but the word is the army is sending another battalion to help retake the city. When the fighting begins, it's going to get bad. Real bad."

Melody shot me a worried look. "Does that mean mom has to stay here?"

"I'm afraid so," I said.

A loud explosion shook the building and we all jumped in fright and turned toward the windows to see a giant blue cloud of gas rise up.

"Oh, no," Sarah said as she walked over to the window and put her hand on the glass.

"What is it?" asked Megan, joining Sarah's side and peering out the window with her.

"That color," Sarah said. "It's the same color as the stuff Dr. Castle injected me with."

"He's aerosolized it," Paul said. He ran his fingers through his afro and added a subdued, "Fascinating."

Another blast went off in another section of town, inside the walls. And more blue gas. This was followed by three more bombs going off all across town. Slowly, that deadly blue gas which was the wicked brainchild of Dr. Castle, slowly filled the air. In an ironic twist, the tall concrete walls of the protective barrier only helped to contain it, becoming a lethal prison instead.

Just then, the hospital alarm went off and we looked at one another and instinctively knew that we needed to leave.

"Come on," Jen said, "Follow me."

We raced down the hallway toward the elevator, but as we approached, the elevator dinged, its doors slid open, and blue gas seeped out into the hallway along with several people who stumbled out of the elevator coughing and hacking.

We slid to a halt in the corridor. We looked back and then, from the sprinklers, blue gas begin to seep out, slowly flowing out of the sprinkler system and raining down death all around us.

Hospital staff and patients alike began coughing and falling over.

"Don't breathe it in," I shouted.

"The stairwell," Billy Bardem said.

We raced to the stairwell, and to our great relief it hadn't been contaminated by the gas. We hopped and skipped down four flights of stairs as fast as we could and burst into the main lobby. It was already filling with lethal blue gas too, and I saw my mom helping a disabled man try to get to the main entrance.

"Mom!" I shouted. "We've gotta go!"

"What's going on, Travis?"

"It's Dr. Castle," Sarah said. "This is the same stuff he poisoned me with. But much more lethal."

"Go!" My mom pointed at the main entrance. "Go before they lock this place down and close the emergency shutters.

A second alarm began to ring and a red light on the wall started flashing. When my mom saw this, she handed me the old man and said, "Hurry."

We all filed into the main entrance as more blue gas began to leak into the main lobby. My mom went back in to grab another patient, covering her face with her arm, she dashed into a cloud of gas. It swirled around her as she disappeared into it.

"Mom!" Melody shouted, turning back to chase her down. But Billy intercepted her, scooped Melody up by her waist, and tossed her onto his shoulder.

"Thanks," I said, as he carried my sister out of the hospital.

Sarah, Megan, Jen, Mitch, and Paul all filed out alongside a throng of other people making a mad-dash to escape the hospital, just then the shudders began to lower.

Hanging back, I called out for my mother. "Mom!" I shouted, cupping my hands over my mouth. "Mom! We've gotta go!"

Standing at the main entrance, I looked up and gauged the exact moment I'd need to dive through the entrance to escape. Luckily, just at the shudders came down halfway, my mom reappeared, carrying an old woman in her arms.

Naturally, my mom being a petite woman, struggled to carry another person roughly her same weight. But she got to me just as the shudder was shoulder high, and handed the old woman off to me.

Megan was already returning to the entrance to check on me and took the old lady. My mom turned to go back one more time perchance to try and rescue at least one more person, but I reached out and caught her hand.

"Mom," I said. "It's too late. You have to let them go."

"No," she said. "There's still time." She jerked her

hand away from me, and with a sad look, began to slowly turn back into the blue gas when, suddenly a large black man appeared out of nowhere and shoved my mom into my arms.

"Get her out of here," Mr. Anders said. With another shove, he pushed us through the wall and then pushed the doors closed just as a gust of newly released gas flooded into the lobby.

"Dad!" Paul screamed. He ran to the doors and tried to pry them open, but Mr. Anders shook his head and held the doors tight.

"No, son," Mr. Anders said, shaking his head. The gas flooded all around him and covered his ankles. Just then, Mrs. Anders appeared by her husband's side, and wrapped her arm around his.

"We love you, Paul. Help your friends. Stay alive. And don't worry about us. Jesus will be watching out for all of us.

"Mom! Dad!" Paul cried out, pounding the glass.

It took everything Mitch and I had to pry Paul away from the glass doors. As we dragged him away, we saw the blue gas engulf his parents.

That's when the shutters dropped entirely, trapping everyone unfortunate enough to remain inside.

Paul shoved us off of him and then slowly sank to the ground. Sitting on the pavement in front of the hospital entrance, Paul sobbed like I'd never seen anyone sob before. It was as if every single tear was made of pure anguish. Anguish he felt over the loss of his parents.

"Paul," my mom said, reaching down and taking his arm. "We've got to go now."

"Just leave me," Paul said, wiping his nose with the back of his hand.

My mom wasn't wrong though, we needed to go. More explosions erupted throughout the city and more blue gas flowed into the streets all around us.

People panicked and screamed and a van and a car crashed no farther than fifty feet from us.

We looked all around for a clear exit, but our path was blocked by blue gas on all sides.

"We're trapped," Mitch said.

"Thanks for pointing out the obvious," Melody said.

Just when we thought there wasn't any hope, a massive, armored transport shot through a cloud of blue gas and screeched to a stop next to us. The passenger side armored door opened and Sergeant Naomi Renteria-Rodriguez leaned over and shouted, "Get in!"

"Right," Billy said, opening the back of the armored vehicle. "Everyone, this way!"

"You don't have to tell me twice," Mitch said, climbing into the vehicle.

Before the rest of us could get into the vehicle, we heard barking and turned to see Sif, our trustworthy golden lab, appear from out of nowhere.

"Sif!" Jen shouted. "Come here, girl!"

Sif raced up to us and was the first to hop into the back of the transport. How she managed to avoid all the toxic gas and still find us was beyond me, but this dog had more lives than a cat.

My mom hopped in the front with Naomi and the rest of us piled into the back of the armored transport.

Megan and I shoved Paul in after Mitch, and Sarah, Melody, and Billy climbed in after. I helped Megan up and, resting my hand on the door, I glanced back one last time to see a massive blue cloud engulf the entire front of the hospital.

I was about to climb in when, through the

smoke, I thought I saw a figure. I stared long enough to see a familiar shape emerge from the smoke. It was a man in a gas mask and a long white medical coat.

Dr. Castle stood staring at me from behind his hideous gas mask, and I merely reached out and flipped him the bird.

"Travis, let's go!" Billy said, reaching out a hand. I took it and he hoisted me up into the back of the transport. I pulled the door shut behind me and quickly sat down beside Megan as Billy reached over and pounded the divider twice, letting Sergeant Rodriguez know we were all safe and secure.

The vehicle lurched forward and we almost toppled over as the massive tires took purchase and tore away from the hospital.

Entering a blue haze, which we could see out of the small visor sized windows, we shared worried glances.

"At least this transport is sealed air tight," Mitch said with a nervous laugh. "It is air tight, isn't it?"

Nobody had any answers for him, so we rode in silence. We rode until we left the confines of the twenty foot walls and shot out of the massive blue cloud that had settled onto the walled-off city.

Breaking free of the poisonous blue haze, the armored vehicle screeched to a halt and we all got out, except for Paul who was still numb from his parent's death. While Paul stayed in the vehicle, the rest of us stepped out into the middle of the street as we looked back at what remained of the settlement.

"All those people," my mom said.

Foot up on the door plate, Sergeant Naomi Rodriquez got on her radio and was trying to get in touch with command, but all she was getting was static. "Someone is jamming my signal," she said.

"Could it be Dr. Castle?" asked Megan. She put her hands on her hips and pushed out her chest, stretching her back perchance to get rid of any unnecessary tenseness.

"I wouldn't put it past him," Sarah replied.

"Who's Dr. Castle?" Naomi asked. She put her two way radio down, giving up hope of ever receiving any reply, and turned to face us.

"The man in the gas mask," I said. "You saw him right?"

"Yeah," Naomi replied. "I saw him in the rearview mirror as we pulled away. Honestly, I didn't know what to make of it."

"He's the one behind all of this. That blue poisonous mist is his doing. He's the one who killed all those people."

Naomi's gaze grew hard and her dark brown eyes smoldered with the fury of a soldier who'd just lost her entire unit. "If you know who did this," Naomi said, pointing back at the blue hazed engulfed city, "You have to tell me. And start from the beginning."

Before I could relay the story of our harrowing encounter with the mad doctor, there was a loud cry and the sound of thunder. But it wasn't thunder. It was the stampede of two hundred aliens.

They charged into the city and over the wall and the blue gas did nothing to deter them. They were completely immune to it. In fact, everything that Dr. Castle had told us had been a lie. The gas didn't negatively affect the aliens at all. In fact, it seemed to have the opposite effect and drew them to it.

That's when I realized that the doctor wasn't trying to save humanity from the aliens. He was trying to help the aliens by recreating their atmosphere—which was toxic to us.

"Hey, Mom," Naomi said, turning toward our

mother. She address my mom as "Mom" with a capital "M" since she didn't know her name yet. But, in all our minds, my mom was "Thee Mom," and the title seemed fitting.

"My name is Emily. Emily Mahoney. Please, call me Em."

"Right," Naomi said. "Em it is." She tossed the keys to the armored vehicle through the air and my mom caught them. "You get these kids to safety, Em. It's up to you now."

"Wait," I said. "Where are you going?"

Sergeant Naomi Rodriguez drew her sidearm and pulled the slide back. After cocking her gun, she glanced over her shoulder and replied, "I'm going to go see about a serial killer."

"You won't survive ten minutes in there," Billy said.

Naomi smiled and then went over to the side of the armored vehicle and slapped the latch on a side compartment, and a panel opened up. Reaching into the cubby, she pulled out a gas mask.

"Don't worry about me, kid. I've got this." With that, Naomi pulled the gas mask on and turned back toward the city.

"She is aware that there's like a thousand aliens swarming the city, right?" asked Mitch. He shot us a worried look, but all we could do was shrug.

"I'm actually more worried about her gas mask," Billy said. "It hasn't even been field-tested with the alien ozone. There's no guarantee that it will mitigate the effects of the gas toxins."

"I guess that's a risk she's willing to take," I said.

The truth was, we had no clue how much of a bad ass Naomi really was. But it was clear that she wasn't afraid. Which meant she was either completely insane or suicidal.

"I'll say this much," Melody said, "she's got balls the size of mother flippin' King Kong's."

"Alright, enough chit chat, everyone," my mom interjected. "Let's get out of here while we still can."

We all filed back into the armored transport, but, this time, Melody chose to sit up front with our mom. I could hear them through the cabin wall arguing about when it was or wasn't appropriate to bring up King Kong's balls. It would have been much funnier had we been in a better mood. But as it was, we were all feeling a bit down.

As my mom got the transport going, I settled

into my seat next to Megan, she reached over and took my hand. Jen, who sat on my right, merely rested her head on my shoulder.

Across the aisle, Billy leaned against the corner closest to the cab and stared vacantly at the floor as he stroked Sif's golden fur. At the same time, Sarah, who sat to Billy's right, scooted closer to Paul and rubbed his back, giving him what little comfort she could. Mitch sat on the end of the bench, gazing at all of our faces.

"Well, spit it out," I said, recognizing the look in Mitch's eyes.

"We should have never left Woodridge," he said. "I mean, I would have rather taken my chances there. At least then our parents wouldn't have been taken, and Paul's mom and dad would still be alive."

"And we'd all be dead, you dipstick," Megan said.

Mitch shot his sister a hurt look and then began to cry. "I just can't take this anymore. It's all bullshit."

Megan looked at me, her face changing to genuine concern and crossed the aisle and sat down next to her brother. Giving him a big hug, she whispered, "I'm sorry. I sometimes forget you're still just a kid."

"We're all just kids," I said.

"Not anymore," Billy said. He then sat up and looked at us all. "You don't' survive literal Hell and then come out with your innocence intact. For better or for worse, we've all been changed. Heck, the whole world is different now. But, if we want to survive in this new world, we have to be strong. We can no longer afford to cling to childish things."

A lingering silence forced us to sit with Billy's words and really take our time to process them.

After a while, Paul looked up, and, speaking for the first time in about an hour of complete silence, asked, "Travis, where in the world is your mom taking us?"

"I have no clue," I replied. "I guess we'll just have to wait and see."

Several hours later, we arrived at a cabin a few miles outside of Sturgeon Bay, Wisconsin, up near Potawatomi State Park.

We filed out of the back of the transport once my mom turned off the engine, dog and all. My sister, Melody, hopped out of the front seat and joined us. She knelt down to give Sif lots of love and scratches.

"We're here," my mom said, turning toward a massive three story cabin that looked out across the entire north section of Sturgeon Bay.

"And where is here, exactly?" Jen asked.

"My colleague's cabin," mom replied.

"By colleague, she means lover," Melody teased, her little brown eyes looking up at us. A devious smile had formed on her lips.

Since the cat was out of the bag, my mom exhaled and then informed us, "Ex-lover, to be precise." Then, turning toward my sister, added, "And that was supposed to be our little secret, young lady."

"What?" Melody asked, pretending not to remember that she'd been sworn to secrecy. Deflecting, she pointed at me and said, "Travis knew, too."

"Knew what?" I asked.

My mom sighed, and then turned toward me. Placing her hands on my shoulders, she looked me in the eyes and said, "You know those medical conferences that I'd been going to every month for the past year or so?"

"Yeah. What about them?"

"Well, I wasn't actually going to any conferences. I was coming up here with Doctor Campbell."

"The gynecologist?" I asked.

"More like gyno-lover," Melody stated.

"Young lady!" my mom gasped, out of exasperation. "Would you kindly zip it?"

Mom met my gaze again and, feeling embarrassed, said, "I'd just been so lonely recently. So, yes, I have a secret boyfriend and maybe I shouldn't have kept it from you. But I didn't know how serious it was and didn't want to disrupt our whole family dynamic if it wasn't going anywhere. And, well, now… here we are."

My mom put her hands on her hips and turned to look at the cabin.

"So, where's Dr. Campbell now?" asked Mitch.

"I don't know," mom replied, letting out a sigh. "He's probably dead."

Jen laughed and then caught herself, covered her mouth with her hands, and looked at all of us with wide eyes full of surprise. "Sorry, it's just the way she said it was kind of funny. So, casual. It caught me off guard."

"I figured if he was still alive he'd find his way here. But, as you all can clearly see, he's nowhere to be found," my mom said. "So, God only knows."

"Well, we're all together now," I said.

"No we're not," Paul muttered. "My parents aren't here. And, if you hadn't realized, Jimmy isn't here either."

"Oh, crap," Mitch said. "In all the chaos, we forgot to go get Jimmy."

"Could he have survived that?" Sarah asked. She looked over at my mom, who thought for a few seconds, and then her eyes lit up.

"Possibly," she said. "Whenever the hospital is locked down, the intensive care unit is hermetically sealed off."

"So that gas wouldn't have gotten in there?" asked Billy.

"I don't know, I mean, it runs on a totally separate system. So, there's a good chance Billy is fine."

"If that's true," I said turning to look down the dirt road that wound its way down the hill and toward the city. "We have to go back for him. We owe him that much."

"I owe him my life," Jen said.

"As do I," Megan said, remembering that time Jimmy saved us from the rogue soldier.

"We all owe him," Billy added. "If it wasn't for him and his fireworks at Fort Liberty, we'd all be worse off, if not dead."

"That settles it, then," my little sister chimed in. "As big as an idiot as he is, he's our idiot. He's a Renegade. And Renegades don't leave other Renegades behind."

"Renegades?" asked our mom.

"The Renegades of Summer," I said.

We all turned and stared off into the distance. Although I didn't know what everyone was thinking, I knew that it couldn't be too different from what was going through my own mind.

Tomorrow was going to be one Hell of a wild day. Tomorrow we'd embark upon the most important rescue mission any of us had been on since the alien invasion and the near complete downfall of civilization. Tomorrow would mark the start of Operation Save "Mad Dog" Jimmy Polson.

6

REBELLION
PART 6: RESCUE MISSION

BY THE TIME WE RETURNED TO DOWNTOWN Chicago, on our journey back to Northwest Memorial Hospital to rescue Jimmy, the blue vapor had dissipated. Luckily, the Windy City lived up to its nickname and had cleared out the toxic gas before our arrival. But what it left behind were six hundred dead bodies.

In one fell swoop, Dr. Castle had become the single most prolific mass murderer in the history of the world. Which meant we had to be extra cautious to avoid running into him again.

Melody, Sif, Mitch, and Paul stayed back at the cabin while Sarah, Jen, Megan, Billy and I returned to rescue Billy. We figured that Paul wouldn't want to come back here let alone risk seeing the bodies of his deceased parents. And Mitch was already having trouble grappling with all the death.

It was clear that Melody needed my mom and my mom needed something to keep her mind off of everything that had gone down. Whether she wanted to admit it or not, Melody was the perfect distraction. Throw in a dog and two emotionally distraught teenage boys, and my mom had enough on her plate to keep her distracted indefinitely.

Megan drove the armored transport into the city and slowed down as we passed through the gates of the walled-off section. Coasting along at ten miles per hour, and being extra careful not to run over any of the human corpses, we kept our eyes peeled for Hunter Killer aliens, Scouts, Dr. Castle, or any potential survivors. But there wasn't a single living soul in sight, extraterrestrial or otherwise. All we saw were countless remains of the deceased.

I don't know why, but big cities that were turned into ghost towns always seemed extra creepy to me. That aside, it allowed us to move quite freely though the city and we arrived at the hospital in no time.

Parking next to the side entrance emergency doors, we all got out and cautiously entered the hospital. Once inside, it took of a couple of minutes to find the sign that pointed to the intensive care unit.

Carefully stepping over dead bodies, we wound through the corridors until we came to a sealed off portion of the building.

"He's got to be in here," I said, touching the wall panel. It required a hand print to open the door and Billy and I looked around the room, checking to see which dead bodies might be a doctor.

"Found one," Megan said, hoisting up a guy by his underarms from behind a large potted plant.

Billy and I rushed over and helped her carry him over to the door. Sarah grabbed his hand and flopped his arm over so that his hand fell right onto the scanner. The scanner activated and then buzzed, flashed red, and remained locked.

"Press it down flat," Jen suggested.

Sarah nodded and then placing her hand onto the dead man's hand, she flattened it against the glass plate of the scanner. It scanned the man's biometrics again, but this time it turned green and chimed a happy little tone.

The glass sliding doors hissed, as the vestibule

between us and the other section of the building decompressed. The doors then began to slide open but got stuck when they were only an inch and a half apart.

Jen raised her boot and kicked the glass doors, dislodging them and they slid the rest of the way open.

"My hero," I said. I smiled at Jen who winked at me and then headed into the ICU.

When I turned around Megan was staring at me suspiciously. "What?" I asked.

"I thought I was your hero."

"You are!" I said. "You'll always be my hero."

"Whatever," she said, pouting. She tried to brush past me, but I caught her by the arm and stopped her.

"Hey, if you don't want me to talk to Jen, I won't. I need you to know that you're the only woman for me. Forever and always."

"Only till she lets you go," Jen said from the other side of the room. "And when she does… I'll be there to catch you and make you mine."

"There not a snowballs chance in Hell I'd ever let you have Travis," Megan said.

Jen merely laughed away Megan's words. "We'll

see," she said. "We'll see."

"As much as we all love Travis," Sarah interrupted, "we need to find Jimmy."

"I think we should split up and look for him," Billy said. "There's three main wings. North, East, and West," he informed, pointing at the long corridors. "The southern exit merely leads back into the E.R. But he has to be here somewhere. I just know it."

Jen skipped up to Megan and said, "We girls will take the east wing. Maybe have some overdue girl talk." She then smiled at me and pulled Megan down the hall with her. Megs looked back at me, a confused look on her face, and all I could do is laugh.

"I guess I'll take the west wing," Billy said, and departed from our current location and went to search for Jimmy on his own.

I looked over at Sarah. "I guess that just leaves you and me."

Sarah linked her arm around mine and smiled. "At long last, the Baby Sitter and the Prodigal Son join forces to mount daring rescue mission."

"What do you think they're talking about?" I asked Sarah, looking down the east hallway at Megan and Jen, who seemed to be getting along for once.

"Oh, they're most definitely talking about you," Sarah said.

"Is that a good or a bad thing?" I asked.

Her face turned cold if not perhaps slightly concerned, and she looked me right in the eyes. Placing both hands on my shoulders, as though she were going to part with some words of wisdom, she said, "Oh, you poor innocent thing. They're going to eat you alive."

"Eat me alive? What?!"

Sarah laughed and pulled me along with her.

About an hour later, Sarah and I returned to the ICU's main lobby and we found Megan and Jen waiting for us at the nurse's reception area. Jen was sitting on the reception desk, legs crossed.

"What'd you find?" Megan asked us.

"Nothing," Sarah replied. "What about you guys?"

"Same. A whole lot of nothing. I hope Billy's having better luck than we are," I said. I turned toward the north wing and suggested, "Maybe we should help him?"

"Yeah," Sarah said, nodding her head. "I agree

with Travis. We finished quickly because we worked in teams, but it'll take Billy twice as long if we sit here twiddling our thumbs."

Jen hopped down off the desk and said, "I'm game."

Not wasting another moment, we all headed up the north wing of the hospital together in search of Billy and, with a bit of luck, Jimmy. We checked every room all the way till the end, but there was no signs of Jimmy or Billy anywhere.

We all started calling out to him. "Billy!"

"Billy Bardem!"

"Backwoods, where the heck are you?"

"Billy!" Sarah hollered down the corridor. We all waited for a response, but there was only the echo of our own voices vibrating up and down the empty hallways. "Billy!" she shouted, again.

Just then, the south wing hermetically sealing doors slammed shut, the hospital alarm went off, and blue gas began seeping out of the ceiling tiles.

"It's a trap!" I shouted.

Sarah looked around and noticed that the only room that wasn't filling with gas was the detachable sauna that sat in the corner of the rehabilitation and physical therapy room.

"Over here!" she shouted. We followed her to the sauna and she opened the door and ushered us inside. "You'll be safe in here."

Once inside, she shut the door from the outside and then wedged a mop handle between the door and the wall so we couldn't get out.

"What are you doing?" asked Megs, tears welling up in her eyes as she ran to the glass window.

"There's something I need to tell you. All of you. I'm immune to the gas."

"Immune?" Megan asked. "What are you talking about, Sarah?"

"The other day, when we were trapped on the fifth floor and you all ran to the stairwell. A sprinkler head went off above me and rained blue gas. I inhaled a lot of it. But… nothing happened. It had no effect on me, even as people were dropping like flies all around me."

"Why didn't you say something?" asked Megan, touching her hand to the glass.

Sarah placed her hand up against Megan's, only a thin plate of glass separating them. "I didn't want to cause anybody to worry. Things were crazy enough without me stopping to say, hey, everyone... I think I have superpowers."

Megan laughed. "That's just like you... always thinking of others before yourself."

Sarah smiled, a look of determination settling onto her face. "I'm going to find Billy, if it's the last thing I do," she stated.

More blue gas erupted all around Sarah, engulfing her fully. She kept her hand on the window and replied, "I love you, Megs. I love all of you."

"We love you, too," Megan replied, a tear trickling down her cheek. With that, Sarah pulled her hand away from the glass, backed into a gaseous blue haze, and disappeared from sight.

"I hope she finds them," I said.

"I hope so too," Megan replied.

A half an hour went by and Megan was pacing back and forth so much so that I had to reach up and stop her. "Megs. Megs, what are you doing?"

"I'm just bored, is all. I tend not to be able to stand still for long stretches of time. I need to be doing something."

Leaning forward, I placed my elbows on my

knees and clasped my hands together in front of my face. "Speaking of not doing anything, how long do you think we need to stay in here before it's safe out there?"

"At least an hour. Maybe two, just to be safe," Jen said.

"Wow. Two hours." I scooted closer to Megan and let out a sigh. "I mean, two minutes already feels like an eternity here. I'd hate to know what two hours is like."

"It won't be that bad," Megan said. "There's a lot we could do in two hours."

"Like what?" I asked.

"Actually, I can think of something we could do," Jen teased, grinning at me and winking. "But I promised Megs here I wouldn't steal her man."

"What?" I asked, not following whatever it was she was talking about.

"I can't have you," Jen said, leaning forward and articulating her words more clearly so that they would sink into my thick skull. "Not until Megan has thoroughly ravished you first," she said.

Megan rolled her eyes. "You won't let this go will you?"

"Let what go?" I asked. I of course understood the not-so-hidden inuendo now, but why it was even a topic up for discussion was still illuding me.

"During our girl talk, I may have inadvertently overshared and told Jen we haven't had sex yet. Not that it's any of her business." Megan placed a worried hand on my thigh and quickly added, "Please don't be mad at me."

"I'm not mad. I honestly don't mind," I said. "You can talk about that stuff all you want. It doesn't bother me."

"I just didn't want to make you feel uncomfortable is all," she added. "Because I do care about you and I know that, in time, it will happen. And it will be beautiful."

"Yeah, about that," I said, rubbing my neck as my cheeks flushed. "I really shouldn't feel uncomfortable. I mean, it's totally natural, right? Why be nervous about it? So, I've been thinking, and, well, I think I'm finally ready."

"You are?" asked Megan, trying her best to mask her excitement. She smiled, because deep down inside, I could tell she really wanted to take that next step with me.

"Until now," I shared, "I'd been too shy to really commit to giving you a clear answer either way. But now I'm ready to tell you exactly how I feel."

"Please know, Travis, no matter what your answer is, I'll still cherish you."

"Yeah, I mean, I've been giving it a lot of thought. And, well, I want to." Megan's eyes lit up and her ears were burning with anticipation as she eagerly waited for what I'd say next. "I mean, as long as Jen's offer is still on the table. I'd love to have a threesome with you both."

Megan gasped. "What? Nooo! That's not... Nope. Uh-uh. I mean... Do you want to die?"

"Deal!" Jen chirped. Growing excited by the prospect, perhaps a little too excited, she immediately reached down and pulled up her shirt halfway, exposing her midriff.

Megan's hand flew out, clutched Jen's wrist, and stopped her mid-strip tease. "That's not what I meant," Megan said. She shot Jen a harsh look and then gave me a perplexed look.

Unable to keep my composer any longer, I burst out laughing. Grabbing my gut, I barely managed to get my words out. "You should have seen the look on your face!"

"Oh, ha-ha, very funny, Travis. Now you'll be lucky if we ever have sex."

"Look, either way, I'm still game," Jen informed us, pulling her shirt back down and brushing out the wrinkles.

Jen sat down beside Megan and slowly exhaled. "Damn, I'm hot and bothered. I swear, you two will be the death of me."

"Us two?" Megan craned her neck and looked at Jen with wild eyes. "How can I put this in a way that you'll understand. You're not a part of this relationship." She pointed and me and her, gesturing that we were the us she was referring to. "You're just a horny Asian chick who can't keep her eyes off of my man."

"He's not complaining," Jen said.

Megan's head slowly swiveled until her fiery gaze was locked onto me like a heat seeking missile. "Now that you mention it, Jen. He has been rather loose about the rules when it comes to flirting with you."

"What?" I laughed. "Leave me out of this."

"Oh, you'd like that, wouldn't you?" Megan said.

"You'd like me to leave you two alone so you could neck behind my back."

"That's not what I meant. You're twisting my words! On purpose!"

Jen raised her hand as if she were a school student about to ask the teacher an important question. "I'm fine with that," she said.

Megan reached over and pressed her index finger against Jen's lips and hushed her. "Shh, sweetie, shhh."

"I… uh…" Stammering, I rubbed the back of my neck, more nervous than I'd ever been. "I don't know what to say."

That's when Megan started laughing. "Oh, you're too much of a push over, Travis. We're just messing with you. We decided to keep messing with you during our girl talk. We're not going to both sleep with you at the same time. That's ridiculous."

"It is?" I asked.

"Damn straight it is. Because you're mine, lover boy. Nobody else's. All mine."

That said, Megs reeled me in and kissed me long and good in front of Jen, to drive her point home. Jen merely seemed to get off on it though and watched with delighted amusement.

Another half an hour passed, and I was once again pacing the floor. "Hey, how long do you think it takes for the poisonous gas to dissipate enough that it wouldn't affect us?"

Both girls, seated next to one another on the bench, looked up and me and simultaneously asked, "Why?"

"Jinx!" Jen said, laughing at the fact that she and Megan were so in sync that it was scary. "And if you say anything, I get to kiss Travis. On the lips."

"Oh, grow up!" Megan said.

"What? You don't think he'd be all over this if he wasn't with you?" asked Jen, running her hands up and down the length of her body and squeezing her own breasts quite aggressively.

"Alright. Fine. I'll prove it." Megan scooted to the end of the bench and waved her hand across the open space on the seat beside her. "Have sex with Travis right here, right now. I'll watch."

I gulped so hard I nearly choked myself. "You'll whuh-what now?"

Megs gestured for Jen to go on ahead and have her way with me. Jen smiled, rose to her feet, and slowly walked toward me. As she drew closer, I drew back, growing self-conscious. I backed all the way up until my back was against the wall.

Jen leaned forward, pressed her body into mine, and pinned me against the sauna door. True to her word, she reached down, drew my chin up, and leaned in for a sultry kiss. Right when our lips were about to touch, the sauna door suddenly jerked open and I tumbled out backwards.

My head hit somebody's shoes and I looked up to see Jimmy "Mad Dog" Polson standing over me.

"What are you guys doing in there?"

"Boy am I glad to see you!" I said.

"Jimmy!" Megan screamed, leaping up and rushing over to Jimmy. She gave him a massive bear hug, picking him up, squeezing him to within an inch of his life, and spinning him around before setting him back down.

Dizzy from the whirlwind that was Megan Powerhouse McIntrye, Jimmy wasn't prepared for Jen Nakamura who walked up to him, placed her hands on his face, and kissed him.

It was no ordinary kiss either. It was full of passion, full of pent up longing, and, most importantly, filled with a whole lot of Jen Nakamura's tongue. The look on Jimmy's face was priceless.

I reached out my hand toward Megan and she gave me a lowdown, under the table five.

Lips locked, Jen held her kiss with Jimmy for as long as she could and then relinquished him and shoved him back. Light-headed, he nearly toppled over because his legs where so weak. Reaching up, he touched his lips and stood in shock, still trying to process what the heck had happened.

"That's for saving me, you pervert! But don't think I'll be making a habit of it."

Jimmy, not knowing how to respond to that, merely nodded.

Megan helped me to my feet and I looked around the room. Noticing that the poisonous gas had all but dissipated, I said, "Hey, guys, we can breathe the air again without dying."

"How'd you find us?" Megan asked, looking over at Jimmy.

Jimmy shrugged. "I don't know. I guess I just heard muffled talking and followed the voices."

"That makes sense," she replied.

"I have a question. How are you not dead?"

"I don't know, Trav," Jimmy replied. "I think I might just be lucky or something."

"Or something doesn't even begin to describe the half of it. But I'm just glad you're alive."

I gave Jimmy a big hug and then we heard a voice say, "Gay."

We spun to find Billy and Sarah standing in the entrance of the physical therapy room.

"Look who I found," she said.

"Where were you?" I asked.

"I was looking for Jimbo," Billy told us, nodding at Jimmy, "when I heard the alarm. Knowing the gas was imminent, I found a large trashcan with a giant clamshell lid and hid inside of it."

"I've been stuck in this sauna, sweating buckets of sweat, and fighting for my life trying not to get mauled by these two femme fatales." With a wave of my hand I gestured from Megan to Jen.

Jen and Megs looked over at me and laughed.

"Yeah right," Megan replied, not even trying to mask her sarcasm. "You wish."

"In your dreams," scoffed Jen.

"Whatever," I said, folding my arms and making

a sour face at both of them.

Once the girls had had their fun torturing Jimmy and me, we decided to head home. Exiting the hospital through a side exit, we did our best to avoid as many dead bodies as possible.

"Hold up," Billy said, walking over to one of the corpses. It had on a military uniform and, unfortunately, looked rather familiar. He knelt down and rolled the person from their side onto their back. When their lifeless body flopped over, Billy put his hand to his mouth and looked away.

"It's Sergeant Rodriguez," Sarah said. A sadness permeated her voice and we all felt it.

"Those are gunshot wounds," Megan said, pointing out that the sergeant had been killed by human hands, not alien ones.

I walked around the room and inspected the area. About twenty feet from the others, I found it. "This might have something to do with it," I said, bending over and picking up a discarded gas mask.

"Her gas mask?" asked Jen. "Why would that have anything to do with it?"

"If the entire area was flooded with lethal toxic gas, why would she have taken it off?"

"She wouldn't have," Billy insisted. "Which means somebody ripped it off of her." Billy found her sidearm, ejected the cartridge, did a quick bullet count and pulled back the slide to see if there was one in the chamber. "She fired off at least five shots."

"Everything laid out to look like she was fending off an alien attack, but the bullet wounds suggest otherwise. Aliens don't use guns," I said.

"Do you think it was him?" asked Megan.

"Dr. Castle?" That would be my guess," said Sarah. "He's definitely a sociopath and since gassing an entire town doesn't seem to give him pause, offing off someone he sees as a threat certainly isn't out of the question."

"It's going to be dark soon," Jimmy observed, glancing up at the sky. "We should probably get back to the hotel."

"Or the cabin," Billy said.

"Cabin? What cabin?"

"Oh, right. You weren't there," I said. "Well, as it turns out, my mom has a cabin up in Wisconsin we didn't know about."

"A secret cabin?" asked Jimmy. "That rocks."

"I don't know if we'd make it back by sundown,"

Jen said looking up at the sinking sun. It was nearly sunset time as it was. "In fact, I don't think we'd make it out of the city by nightfall. So, Jimmy is right. We'll stay at the hotel tonight and in the morning we'll meet back up with Travis's mom, those two nerds, and Melody."

"Nerds?" Jimmy asked.

"Man, you missed a lot," I said. "Mitch and Paul are back. But it's a long story. I'll tell you on the way back to the hotel."

Caught up on all the details, we turned to find our armored ride waiting for us. Billy being Billy, however, stayed back and unbuttoned his black shirt. We paused to turn back and watched him lay it over Naomi as a sign of respect.

Shirtless, Billy caught up to us and the girls whistled and cat-called him as a tease.

"Stud-muffin," Jen said, biting her lip.

Megan whistled and as Billy passed Sarah she slapped him on the butt. He laughed and shook his head as he jogged to catch up to us.

Once we climbed back into the armored transport, Billy open the bench seat, pulled out a package, ripped it open, and found a green military undershirt inside. He slipped it on and it fit him like a glove.

"Here, Travis," Megan said, tossing me the keys to the armored transport.

I caught them and looked down at them resting in my hands. "But I don't know how to drive."

"I'll teach you," Megan said, her grin widening.

Smiling, I nodded and promptly climbed into the driver's seat. With Megan's keen instructions, I fumbled my way through her version of driver's ed, and thirty-five minutes later, we arrived at the Pendry Hotel.

7

REBELLION
PART 7: STRANGE ALLIANCES

Most of the city was either deceased or missing and there wasn't anybody left to run the power grid. Unlike the hospital, which had its own power backup, the Pendry Hotel had gone dark.

Hiking the thirty-three flights of stairs by flashlight took us forty five minutes, every step more excruciating than the last. By the time we got back to the hotel suite, we were drenched in sweat and our legs felt like they were made of rubber.

"I need a bath," I said.

"Me too," Billy added.

"Me three," Megan said.

"I think we all do," Sarah agreed.

Jen and Jimmy nodded.

As per our custom, we all stripped to our underwear and headed to the jacuzzi bathroom.

Luckily, the hot water tank hadn't been fully drained yet and we had one full bath left. As the stream rose from the rippling water, we all sank in and exhaled, releasing our stress and tension with every breath.

There was little to no talking, something rare for our group. Rather, we just soaked—even while still in our underwear—we let ourselves relax and leaned back in the tub and stared up at the ceiling tiles together.

About thirty minutes passed and Jen was the first to get out. Standing up, she grabbed a towel from the rack and began to dab herself dry. Once she was done, she paused in the doorway, her back to us, and let her long raven hair fall across her shoulder. Dropping her towel to the floor and tossing her hair, she glanced back across her bare shoulder, and said, "Hey, Jimmy? You coming or what?"

Jimmy's jaw about hit the floor and we all hooted and whistled as he slowly climbed out of the tup and took Jen's hand. She smiled and then guided him down the hallway to her bedroom.

Sarah and Billy, Megan and I, dried off and headed to the living room. We decided on setting the couch between us, but leaving enough room on either side so that we could each see the fireplace from our respective positions. After getting a fire going, we rolled out our sleeping bags on opposite sides of the couch and laid down.

"So," I said, rubbing the back of my neck nervously. "What do you want to do?"

"I want you to shut up and kiss me," Megan said, a prurient sparkle in her eye.

We kissed. Things grew steamy, and the petting grew intense. Things were happening faster than I could have imagined and I realized, perhaps, this was going to be my first time.

I trusted Megan implicitly to take care of me. Putting my full trust in her, I gave into the moment, because I'd been fighting my feelings for far too long and now, well, I just wanted to enjoy being with her. We were in love, and it seemed wrong to withhold the whole of my love—the physical part—any longer. The mental, physical, and spiritual all had to come together in the moment, because if I couldn't express my love fully, then I feared maybe it wasn't real.

Beyond a group of guys and gals discovering what the birds and the bees were up to, we truly cared about one another. Truly. Madly. Deeply. And

I don't just mean Megan and myself. I mean the whole team. The Renegades of Summer were a clan and over the course of the past two weeks, our bond of friendship had been tempered by the fires of unfathomable adversity.

As for Megan, my sweet Megan, she was everything I could ever want in a girlfriend, in a partner, in a woman. She was beautiful, funny, fiercely protective, and she had a little bit of a nerd streak that complimented my own nerdiness. She was the one I wanted to spend the rest of my life with. Of that, I was sure.

My cheeks flushed, my body quivered, and I focused on the feel of Megan's lips pressing against mine. Of course, the other stuff happened naturally too, but I didn't dare focus on anything else for fear it would overwhelm me.

I can't really describe it beyond the typical metaphorical and poetic stuff that almost all romance poetry springs from. The bottom line was that the depth of our connection seemed endless. And Megan smiled at me, her hair glowing angelic in the firelight, and even with me not knowing what I was doing… it didn't matter. She still loved me for me.

And I felt at home in the embrace of her arms.

Then, in the same way we had started, my cheeks flushed and my body quivered, and I looked up into her ocean blue eyes and whispered, "I love you, Megan Michelle McIntyre."

She fell onto the sleeping bag beside me, panting from the workout she'd given herself, sweat dripping down her neck and chest. She kissed my lips and pulled me into her. "I love you too, Travis. Forever and always. Because you are my everything."

We kissed on last time and fell asleep in each other's arms, much the same way, I imagined, as Romeo and Juliet must have when they began their forbidden romance.

That night, I had the best sleep of my life.

Come daybreak, we slowly roused from our beds and shared knowing glances as we dressed. But we didn't say a word. For us, last night was a sacred coming of age experience. We had gone to bed as boys and had woken up as men. As for the women folk, well, they seemed extra cheerful. And if they were happy then we were happy, as cliché as that sounded.

We sat around the dining table eating dry cereal,

because there was no fresh milk, and the crunching of Honey Nut Cheerios filled the room. Luckily, Jen had stored some bananas in the refrigerator which were still good and paired nicely with our Cheerios.

During all of breakfast we scarcely said more than three words to each other, but there was a lot of stifled giggles, sideways glances, and blushing. Also, it seemed a little weird that we were eating a kids cereal after making the transition into adulthood, but, then again, that's all there was to eat.

After breakfast, we went to the hotel storage room, found more dry cleaning, and changed into entirely new outfits. This time, we aimed to dress the same. So, we dressed in all black. Black shirts, black jeans, black skirts, everything in black.

Jen managed to find a miniskirt and black Gogo boots, which complemented the black tank top she wore. Megan found a button up vest that belonged to a man's suit and put it on minus anything beneath, not even a bra. She also found some bellbottom jeans and bright red Chuck Taylor AllStar sneakers to round out her ensemble.

Sarah, meanwhile, decided to switch things up and found a women's business suit with a matching blazer and a white blouse shirt underneath. It was business chic, the same kind of thing that Princess Dianna would be seen wearing whenever she appeared at public events like Wimbledon or when she adorned the front of magazine covers.

Billy, Jimmy, and myself managed to find three pairs of jeans and matching black Fruit of the Loom t-shirts.

Like Megan, we all decided to find red shoes. Everyone apart from Jen's tactical boots, managed to find red shoes. To complement our dash of color, Jen found a red handkerchief and rolled it up and tied it around her left upper bicep.

Fully dressed, we grabbed our stash of weapons. Jen had her samurai swords, Megan her hockey stick with a machete duct taped to the handle end so that it became a makeshift bayonet. Jimmy fetched himself the baseball bat with nails that Mitch had fashioned back at Billy Bardem's house the day that Woodridge was overrun.

Sarah grabbed Melody's kukri knives and the halter top holster so she could strap them to her back. Melody wouldn't be needing them since she was back at the cabin with mom. While she strapped the blades to her back, I grabbed the dual, red bearded tomahawk hatchets, and a couple of carabiners to create loops that would allow me to holster the axes on my belt.

Speaking of belts, Jimmy went all out finding an oversized Harley Davidson belt buckle.

Armed to the teeth, we were finally ready to make the trek back up to Wisconsin—back to the cabin where my mom, Melody, and our resident nerds Mitch and Paul were all waiting eagerly for our safe return.

Knowing that this might be the last time at the Pendry, we cleaned out any food we could carry, grabbed our sleeping bags and camping gear, and then rode the elevator down to the first floor.

Exiting the hotel, we all stepped outside only to find approximately two hundred aliens standing in a large semicircle around the entrance of the building. They took up most of the street and at the very center of the throng was Lucy.

Everyone dropped their backpacks and drew up their weapons, but I raised my hand and motioned them to stay calm.

"Uh, guys, I don't think this is an attack party.

They could have attacked the building at any time during the night."

"So, what are you saying, Trav?" asked Jimmy. "They've just been waiting out here to… what? Have a friendly chin wag?"

"Actually," I said, looking over at him. "I think that's exactly what they want to do."

"Lucy is psychic," Sarah added.

"And he did give you the visions that warned you about Jen."

"Warned him about Jen? What?" asked Jen.

"Apparently the aliens think you're dangerous," I said, looking to Jen and then pointing a few feet behind her. "You might want to keep a safe distance so they don't get the wrong idea."

"What did you do to piss off the aliens?" Jimmy asked, smiling at Jen Nakamura with a boyish grin.

"I may have killed one of them."

"Bare handed?" Megan asked.

"Basically," Jen said. She did as I suggested and took a couple of steps backward. Jimmy stepped in front of her to let the aliens know that she wasn't an immediate threat.

Once she was behind us, Lucy huffed, and then

slowly approached me. I reached out a hand and Lucy nudged it, like a massive kitten, and then I leaned forward and we touched our foreheads together.

I closed my eyes and in another instant a flood of visions came into my mind. Gasping, I jerked back. I almost lost my footing but Billy was there to catch me and prop me up.

"What did you see, man?" he asked.

"Apparently, there's two factions of aliens. Ones that have decided to co-exist with humans, and those that still want to kill every human on sight."

"I hope these are the non-killing sort," Megan said.

"You and me both, sister," Jimmy said.

"I'm not your sister, dude," Megan said.

"Alright, alright. Don't get your dick all tied up in a knot over it," Jimmy deflected, raising his hands in defeat.

This caused Jen to laugh out loud.

"Oh, that was funny to you was it?"

"Actually, it was," Jen said. "Jimmy is a funny, guy."

"Why thank you, Jen. I appreciate you saying so." Turning to Megan, he added, "At least someone appreciates my sense of humor."

"I think," Billy said, "That in the time you all took to have whatever that conversation was, these aliens could have killed every single one of us. So, clearly, they're not the anti-human kind."

Lucy groaned in the manner I imagine a dinosaur would, and turned back toward the herd. As he did, the rest of the aliens turned and they started heading up the street.

"What are they doing, Trav?" asked Sarah.

"I think they want us to follow them."

"Clearly," Sarah said. "But why?"

"It's not entirely clear. But one of the visions was an arial view of the city. It showed three colors. The walled off area with the hospital was blue. There was red from the north, east, and south, and then yellow from here to the waterfront."

"Why would Lucy show you a vision of a map?"

"I think he was trying to give me a heads up on where the dangerous aliens are."

"If that's the case," Billy said, "then our entire route back up north is blocked."

"That would be my guess too," I said. "There's effectively no way out of the city. It's been completely taken over by the dangerous breed of aliens."

"In that case," Jen said, "Maybe we should follow your alien pet. Because I don't know about anybody else, but I'd rather take my chances with the friendly aliens than the unfriendly ones."

We all agreed and followed Lucy's pack to the DuSable Harbor. There, they led us to the docks where there were an endless choice of boats.

"Awesome!" Jimmy said, running out onto one of the many docks. Rows of boats, nearly all of them white, lined the entire port. "Some of these are borderline yachts!" he exclaimed.

"Try to find one with its keys," I said.

"I'll help," Billy said.

"We will too," Sarah added.

Megan and Jen accompanied Sarah and the girls went up one row of boats while the guys looked up another.

I stayed back and turned to look at Lucy. He approached me while his herd hung back. We touched heads again, and rubbing his giant banana shaped cranium, I said, "Well, this is where we part ways. Maybe forever."

Lucy whined sadly and then nuzzled me, like a

cat would. I staggered back and laughed.

"I'll miss you too, boy. Now, you go back to your family and take care. I'll tell Melody you said goodbye."

Lucy let out a low groan and made a clicking sound I'd never heard before and then turned away and began to head back to the herd.

As he left, I raised my hand and waved goodbye. And, although I wasn't sat, I felt a single tear trickle down my cheek. It wasn't sadness, more like a bittersweet ending.

Lucy had used his herd to help mask our presence from the violent aliens and give us time to escape the city.

"Here!" Jimmy shouted, jingling some boat keys in the air. "I found some!"

A massive sense of relief washed across us and we all gathered on the boat. Jimmy was about to put the keys in and then paused.

"What's the matter," I asked.

He looked at me, a puzzled look on his face. "I don't know how to drive a boat." Looking over his shoulder at everyone else, he asked, "Does anyone know how to drive a boat?"

"I do," Jen said, taking the keys from Jimmy.

"Of course you do," said Megan, folding her arms over her chest. "Ms. Trust Fund here probably goes yachting on the weekends."

"As a matter of fact, we do," Jen said. "At least, we have a boat up by the lake house and we often take it out on the weekends during the summer."

With that, Jen started up the boat and pulled us out into the harbor.

"You might all want to take a seat and get comfortable," Jen said. "Boat trips tend to be rather long and boring."

"How long could it be?" asked Jimmy.

"Well," Jen said, tapping her chin as she thought about it. "Basically, they're twice as slow as cars, even without boat traffic. So, if it took us three hours by car to get from the cabin to the city, we'd basically need to double that."

"Six hours?" gasped Jimmy.

"Six hours weather permitting," Jen replied. "If a storm comes in, we'll have to pull ashore, find a place to dock."

"It'll be fine," Sarah said. "We'll take turns steering the boat so nobody gets tired."

"Why are you headed dead West, though?" asked Billy.

Jen smiled and looked back over her shoulder at him, tossing her silky black hair in a flirtatious manner. "Because, handsome, I don't want those creatures to follow us up the coast." She jutted a thump over her shoulder and we all turned around to see that the entire shoreline of Chicago was swarming with aliens, both good and bad.

"There's so many of them," Jimmy said.

"Oh my God! Look! Over there!" Megan practically screamed, startling nearly every one of us. She pointed a finger at a section of one of the beaches. "Do you see it? It's a baby."

"A what?" Jimmy looked at us, confusion taking over his face. "A human baby?"

"No," Megan replied as he still tried to figure out what she meant. "An alien baby, you idiot."

Sarah ran over to the cubby next to Jen, popped it open, and rummaged through it. "Here," she said, holding up a pair of binoculars. "Use these."

She handed them to Megan who pinpointed the little alien and then handed the binoculars off to Billy. We all took turns looking at the freshly hatched youngling and it was, like all babies, ridiculously cute. It's head was far too big for its little body and its eyes were giant-sized as well.

"Even for an alien," Jimmy said, staring through the binoculars, "I have to admit it's pretty darn cute."

"Maybe that's why they've been so fiercely determined to get rid of all the humans from the city. They were clearing it out to give their young a safe place to live."

"I just had a thought," Sarah said.

"What is it?" I asked.

"Dr. Castle," she replied, not giving us any context. Realizing we were more confused than a rat in a maze, she cleared her throat and clarified. "You know how you and Lucy have this kind of psychic link? What if Dr. Castle met one of the dangerous aliens, but it let him live, and was giving him visions of how to help them?"

"That would mean the aliens are more intelligent than we initially thought," Billy said.

"Even if he was trying to help them," Megan added, "he still tried to kill you. Which doesn't make it right."

"I know that," Sarah said. "But seeing that

youngling got me to thinking. What if they're not violent for violence sake. What if they're just trying to protect their colony?"

"That might not be too far off the mark," I said. "Paul's theory was that their planet was destroyed and they hitched a ride on the planetary debris and sailed through the galaxy until crash-landing on our planet... on Earth."

"We might never know," Billy said. "But I don't like the fact that Dr. Castle is out there. Regardless of his motives, he's a mass murdering psychopath."

"What are you thinking about, hoss?" Jimmy asked.

"I just can't help but have this bad feeling that we're not out of the woods yet. There's a Big Bad Wolf in the woods, and it has seen us."

Sarah reached over and took Billy's hand. "You think he's going to come looking for us?"

"I think as long as he knows that we know what he did, he's going to want to silence us. And for somebody like him, where killing is as easy as breathing to him, he wouldn't hesitate killing anyone of us."

"I won't let that happen," Jimmy said.

Jen nodded in full agreement with Jimmy's assessment. "Jimbo is right."

"What are you thinking?" Megan asked, noticing the Jen had an intense look of concentration on her face.

"I'm thinking, maybe we find this asshole before he finds us and deal with him."

"Are you saying we murder someone?" I asked.

Jen shrugged. "Hey, it's survival of the fittest out here, haven't you noticed?"

"As true as that may be," Sarah said, "nobody is going to be murdering anyone. Of all of us here, I've earned the right to draw the line. We're not killers. But Dr. Castle is, and if we want to be ready for a final showdown with him, we'll need to be prepared."

"That settles it then," I said. "Once we get back to the cabin, will debrief everyone on the situation. And maybe, just maybe, we won't get so caught off guard the next time Dr. Castle shows up with his twisted bag of parlor tricks."

8

REBELLION
PART 8: SUMMER'S END

THE LEAVES ON THE TREES BEGAN TO CHANGE colors, shifting to beautiful gradients of red, yellow, and orange and the coming of autumn marked the end of our long summer. Our year had started out with big plans and even bigger dreams. All of that was dashed by a series of meteor showers that brought with it alien life. And then, almost overnight, society as we know collapsed.

For the past three months, we stayed at the cabin up in Sturgeon, Wisconsin. And the whole time we were there, we never ran into another person outside our close knit group.

During June, July, and August my mother frantically gardened. She taught us all how to garden. And we had planted everything from corn to tomatoes, zucchini to eggplant, bell peppers to cucumbers, snap peas, to the main staple of carrots and potatoes.

My mom also taught us canning so that we could have peaches, pears, and pickles to eat during the winter.

She also made hundreds of cans of chili for us while Billy and I had gone into the nearby woods and hunted several elk which we turned into elk jerky.

In fact, the cabin's wine cellar had been converted into our food cellar, and the entire basement had been remade as a storage facility for all our food items, both scavenged and homemade.

"I can't believe it's already September," Sarah said, lounging on the massive, L-shaped sectional sofa that sat in the middle of a giant living room. A nice wood fire crackled nearby and Billy and I, who'd just returned with some small game, including six rabbits and a cooler full of trout from the lake, and took our things into the kitchen where Jimmy, Mitch, and Paul would gut, clean, and preserve the food.

Sarah sat up and leaned across the back of the couch as she watched us wash up. "You guys realize that you're officially high school students now?"

"That's right," my mom said. "This is the week that classes would be starting. But since you all blew up your school…"

"Mom!" I gasped, shooting her a sharp look. "It wasn't like that."

"I know, sweetie. I'm just teasing." She laughed and grabbed a basket full of laundry and went to the laundry room. Yes, the house was big enough to have its own dedicated laundry room.

She cranked up the gas generator and got it going so she could run the machines.

"Too bad the electricity cut out last month," Megan said. She had her legs up on the coffee table and was sitting in a large armchair reading a book. I glanced at the title and it said, *Pride and Prejudice.*

"Yeah," Sarah sighed, sliding back onto the sofa. "I miss long hot showers." Stretching out, she lay flat on her back and looked up at the A-frame ceiling.

Up on the second floor balcony, Melody and Sif ran by as they played a game of chase through the whole house.

"Hey," I said, drying my hands off with a towel as I came back out into the living room. "Has anybody seen Jen?"

"I thought she headed out this morning on another one of her long scouting trips."

"Hopefully she didn't go too far, this time," Billy said. "Last time we were mounting up to go and track her down when she strolled in half and hour past sundown."

"I'm not scouting today," Jen stated. We turned to see her standing in the doorway of the master bedroom, her face as pale as a ghost.

"Oh, honey," my mom said, racing up to her and checking her forehead with the back of her hand, "you're burning up."

"I think I might be sick," she said. Covering her mouth, her cheeks puffed up and we could tell she'd just vomited into her own mouth. She held up a finger, turned around, and darted into the bathroom.

A few seconds later we heard the toiled flush, the sink turn on, and then gargling.

"Poor thing," my mom said.

"Jimmy," Megan shouted from the living room. "Your girlfriend is sick!"

Jimmy entered the living room from the kitchen and I pointed to the bedroom.

"She's puking her guts out as we speak."

"Thanks, Travis," Jimmy said, patting my shoulder with a friendly thank you as she darted on by. "Jen! I'm coming!"

"I still can't believe she decided to date that kid," Sarah said. "I mean, don't get me wrong. Jimbo is a standup guy. He's just not... dating material."

"Oh, I can believe it," Megan said, without looking up from her book. "That girl is hornier than Ms. Lydia on a Wednesday."

"I don't get that reference," I said, "but I assume it has to do with that book you've been reading?"

"As a matter of fact, yes, Travis. It does." Megan put her feet down and leaned forward in her chair. "You see, Miss Lydia, the youngest of the five Bennet sisters, falls for the charming, but secretly Narcissistic, Mr. Wickham. Her impetuous love causes her to elope with him, a scandal that shakes the entire community, since back then breaking the rigid customs of the Regency era England was one of the biggest societal taboos you could do. But little does she know that Mr. Wickham doesn't really love her because he is harboring a deep seated romantic desire for her second oldest sister, the heroine of the story, Ms. Elizabeth Bennet. But, Ms. Elizabeth won't touch Mr. Wickham with a ten foot pole because she sees right through his womanizing ways and recognizes he's a playboy and a knave."

"So, you're saying that Jimmy is like Mr. Wickham?"

"No!" Megan said, slamming the book closed in her hands. "At his core, Jimmy is a good guy. Mr. Wickham is a womanizing scoundrel. But Jen is more like Ms. Lydia. She is impetuous. Promiscuous. And makes brash decisions." She then reopened her book, leaned back in her chair, and picked up where she left off in her reading.

"I'd better go check on those two," I said. Billy gave me a two-finger salute and I left the room, glancing back to see him take a seat next to Sarah and lean over and kiss her forehead. She smiled and then placed her head in his lap and they sat and watched the fire together.

When I turned the bend and entered the bathroom, Jimmy and Jen were sitting on their knees in front of the toilet, tongue deep in each other's faces.

"Gross!" I said. "She just vomited?"

"You're only young once, Travis!" Jimmy said,

taking the smallest of breathers to relay that apparently vital and necessary information.

"That doesn't make any sense," I told him.

He shrugged and then said, "You don't get it Travis, when you love someone, you love all of them."

"You're so damn romantic," Jen said, grabbing Jimmy by the scruff of his neck and pulling him into her, their lips mashing together. With that, they immediately went back to making out and I took that as my cue to leave them to their canoodling.

Wondering into the kitchen, I checked on Mitch and Paul who were scraping scales off fish while getting into a heated debate of who'd win in a bar fight—a team of Wookies or a team of Klingons.

Granted, I had my own take, but I knew better than to get into it with them since they inevitably would team up against your opinion and argue with you until you got frustrated and gave up.

Leaving them to it, I headed upstairs and checked on Melody who was lying on her bed reading a *Wonder Woman* comic book while Sif sad beside her panting noisily.

"Did you know that same guy who invented the

polygraph machine also created Wonder Woman?" Melody asked me.

"Actually, yes. I did know that."

"Uh-huh," Melody said, sounding rather skeptical. But she left it at that as she was too engrossed in the story and, ignoring my presence, went back to reading her comic.

All things considered, when I told her about Lucy, she took the news fairly well and told me that she knew it wouldn't be the last time we saw him. I didn't know if that was wishful thinking or if Melody knew something I didn't. After all, she had a much stronger psychic link with Lucy than I did.

While upstairs, I decided to go over to the window and look outside. That's when I saw them. An entire armada of military boats floated down Sturgeon Bay, down Lake Michigan, and toward the Windy City.

"Turn off the lights!" I hollered over the railing from the second floor. "Turn off the generator. Draw all the blinds. Now!"

Everyone jumped up and went into action mode. Once we'd darkened the cabin and locked everything down, we all crept over to the main windows and peeked out at the lake.

The military brought in three Coast Guard cutters, including a giant Polar-class icebreaker with a helicopter landing pad and other littoral combat ships. There were five smaller Protector class vessels, an old WWII battleship, long since decommissioned and a couple other non-military boats. That's when a submarine emerged, breaking the crest of the water, and sending out waves all around it.

I could only assume they'd gathered the fleet from all the Maritime museums around the lake, of which there were probably a dozen or more. And now, they were carrying hundreds of soldiers, shipping them down to Chicago to try and retake the city.

"Things are about to go down," Jimmy said.

I nodded, agreeing with Jimmy's sentiment. Things were about to go down and you didn't need to be a rocket scientist to know that it wasn't going to be pretty.

Grabbing my jacket off the hook by the front door, I pulled the keys to the neighbor's Plymouth Voyager minivan out of the pocket and turned to face everyone.

"What are you doing, Travis?" asked my mom, folding her arms and giving me a hard gaze.

"I've got to warn Lucy. I don't care how dangerous it is, but I can't let Lucy be killed in a military blitzkrieg. If I take the car and leave now, I can beat them to the city by at least three hours."

"Even if you get there ahead of them," Megan asked, "how are you going to find Lucy? He could be anywhere in the city."

"I don't know," I said, shaking my head. "But I have to try. I can't let him die for nothing."

"In that case," Billy said, picking his shotgun up from where he left it earlier, "I'm coming with you."

"Me too," Megan said, standing up. She placed her book on the coffee table and stepped forward just as Sarah stood up.

"That makes two of us," Sarah said, volunteering herself for the mission.

Although I could see that Jen wanted to come with us, before she could say anything she ran to the end of the couch, bent over the waste basket, and hurled into it.

Wiping specs of puke from the corner of her mouth, she said, "I'll get my things."

"Like Hell you are, young lady," my mom said, walking right up to Jen and grabbing her by the arm. "Where you're going is straight to bed."

"Guys," Jimmy said, his eyes growing soft and apologetic. "I think I'm going to sit this one out. As much as I'd like to go with you, I really think I need to stay here and take care of my girl. At least, until she's better."

"No worries," I said. "You've gotta take care of your girl. That goes without saying."

"He's not my..." Jen raised the waste basket and hurled again. *blehhhrrg*

I looked over at Mitch and Paul.

Mitch shook his head. "I'm sorry, guys. I've had my fill of death for a lifetime. I think Paul and I will take Jimmy's lead and sit this one out too."

Paul looked at Mitch and then us. Not saying a word, he walked over and grabbed his jacket off the wall. "Speak for yourself, Mitch. But I'm bored out of my mind here and I think this is just the medicine I need to get me out of my slump."

Mitch turned red in the face, anger rising up from the feeling of betrayal he obviously felt. But he didn't complain. He just folded his arms across his chest and said, "I get it. Don't die out there."

"If we're not back in twenty-four hours," I said, "Send in the calvary."

"Who's the calvary?" asked my mom.

"You are," I said, smiling at her.

On that note, I opened the front door and Billy, Paul, Sarah, Megan and I piled into the 1986 Plymouth Voyager and I started it up.

"I'm so glad I taught you how to drive," Megan said, settling into the passenger seat next to me.

"Me too," I agreed, leaning over and giving her a quick peck on the lips.

Sarah and Billy sat in the middle row of the minivan which left the back seat all for Paul. They watched as I twisted the key and started the car. With a high-pitched whine, a grinding sound, and a few needless clunks, the engine finally came to life.

Getting it out on the open road, the engine shook out all of its hiccups and started to sound normal again. Driving about seventy the whole way, without headlights to ensure we weren't spotted, we got to the city in record time.

As we entered city limits, I slowed the van to about twenty miles per hour and we eased through the empty streets.

"Where do you think Lucy is?" Sarah asked from the back seat.

"I don't know. I think our best bet is to head to the Pendry Hotel, drive around there for a bit, and look for him. I'm open to any ideas though."

"Have you guys noticed anything strange?" asked Megan as she peered out the window.

"No, why?" I asked.

"All the dead bodies from Dr. Castles attack… they're all gone."

"Do you think the aliens moved them?" asked Billy.

"It would make logical sense," Paul informed, pushing up his glasses, "rotting human bodies are a terrible biohazard. Our species carries more communicable diseases than any other animal outside of bats and rats."

Out of nowhere, one of the larger aliens rammed the van, jolting us and causing immediate panic. We all screamed, the girls loudest out of the bunch except for Paul, who screamed higher pitched than anyone even though he had the deepest voice.

"Step on it, Travis!" Megan shouted, bracing

herself by grabbing the dashboard and her door handle.

I floored it, the van sputtered, and then gradually picked up speed. It wasn't exactly a Farrari.

The alien managed to keep pace, ramming us with its shoulder a second time. But as I got it up past forty miles per hour the alien began to fall behind.

It slowed to a trot, and then stopped in the middle of the street and squawked loudly at us, as if it were chastising us for our reckless driving.

"Do you think it'll warn the others?" Paul asked as he twisted around in his seat to watch the alien shrink away in the rearview window.

"Being telepathic," I said, my hands gripping the steering wheel so tightly my knuckles turned white, "my bet is that they already know we're here."

"Turn on the headlights, Travis," Sarah said from the back seat.

I did as Sarah asked and as soon as the road lit up so did a wall of aliens.

"Holy crap on a stick!" I shouted as I hit the brakes. The minivan's wheels locked and we skidded to a stop, the whole van sliding sideways a bit before fully lurching to a halt.

Everyone got tossed around, but we were all wearing our seatbelts so nobody got hurt apart from the seatbelt rash left on our bodies.

"Do you think these are the mean aliens or the nice aliens?" asked Paul. He pushed up his glasses and leaned forward in his seat to get a better look out of the front windshield.

"That's a good question," I said. But the truth was, I had no clue. And, regardless of which aliens these were, it seemed we'd come to the end of the line.

REBELLION
EPILOGUE

BEFORE WE COULD DECIDE WHAT TO DO, ONE of the aliens leaped into the air and pounced on the hood of the van, crushing it in. His other foot landed on the windshield, fracturing our glass. Everyone screamed again as the beast pressed its snout against the glass and roared at us.

"That's enough, Sayathong," a human voice called out. The alien stomped angrily on the windshield, fracturing it some more, but then heeded the human words and hopped off and returned to the herd.

Several of the aliens stepped aside, as did the ones behind them, and this concession continued all the way down the line revealing a long narrow path with a dark figure—a human figure—standing at the very end of the alien passageway.

The mysterious figure walked toward us and,

stepping into the light of our headlights, Dr. Castle emerged.

"Not him again," Billy muttered.

Dr. Castle reached out to the alien that had accosted up and patted its head. "Good girl, Sayathong. Very good," he said and then she turned around and rejoined her brothers and sisters.

"Stay here," I said, opening the car door. I stepped out, keeping my eye on the aliens for any signs of movement. But they didn't seem to get overly excited and kept their rank and file.

Megan opened her door and got out too, and I looked over at her and asked, "What are you doing? I said to stay in the car."

"To Hell with that, Travis. I'm not letting you do this alone. You and I are a team. Forever and always."

I smiled at her and nodded. Megan would have my back till the end of time, if need be. She was my ride or die. And for that, I loved her even more.

"Can you believe she was no larger than a baby elephant a few months ago?" Dr. Castle asked, addressing Megan and me. "And now, this lovely girl is the size of an African rhinoceros." He patted the side of Sayathong, as one would pat the side of their horse.

Megan and I turned toward Dr. Castle and scanned the entire litany of alien faces. There were hundreds of them. Maybe even thousands.

"As interesting as all that is, Dr. Castle, you have to evacuate the city. Get these creatures to safety."

"That's not how they operate, I'm afraid," he replied. "They're ridiculously territorial, and they like being near the fresh water. Chicago is their home now, and we will just have to accept that fact."

"You don't understand," I said. "The military is coming down the pike. And they're going to take the city."

"They can try," the doctor said, not feeling any sense of immediate worry.

"They're bringing battleships with sixteen inch canons. They'll be able to level the entire city."

"I doubt that very much."

"Are you willing to let these creatures die?" I shouted, pointing at all the aliens.

Dr. Castle drew out a Sig Sauer 9 mm handgun and pointed it at me. Megan took a step forward and he merely swung his aim toward her, causing her to stop and take a few steps back.

Then, twirling the gun in his hand so that the handle was generously offered to me, Dr. Castle said, "Take it."

"What?" I asked.

"Don't do it, Travis. It's a trick."

"It's no trick, Travis," the doctor replied, using my name for the first time and grinning at me in a very creepy sort of way. "I promise you. Take it and try to shoot me."

I stepped forward and cautiously took the gun from him and then backed up. "You want me to shoot you?"

"I want you to *try* and shoot me," he corrected.

I raised the gun and pulled back the slide. "Fine," I said. "You'll be doing the world a favor."

I held the gun, aiming it right at his chest, but I couldn't bear killing anyone. That's when Megs marched over to me, snatched the gun out of my hand, and then turned and fired three rapid shots at Dr. Castle's head.

The bullets stopped inches from his nose, caught in midair by a pink energy barrier. We watched in amazement as each of the aliens five eyes glowed bright pink.

"Don't worry about the aliens, Travis. As you can see, with their psychic powers, they're perfectly safe from any outboard threats. Including, I think you'll find, the full arsenal of the United States Military."

Suddenly a spot light lit us up from the waterfront and a Coast Guard Interceptor got on the megaphone and said, "This is the United States Coast Guard. Put down your weapons and walk toward the water. I repeat, lay down your arms and walk toward the water."

Dr. Castle looked at me, smiled and then turned to his favorite alien. "Sayathong, my love, would you be so kind as to show those gentlemen who really rules this nest?"

Sayathong, the alien, snorted and trotted toward the water and the boat floating a hundred feet offshore. When the Coast Guard saw the alien coming, they didn't hesitate to open fire. But, sure enough, just like the bullets from our gun that had been stopped, the same mysterious pink energy field caught the Coast Guards bullets and kept them suspended in air.

Sayathong planet her back feet and fanned her

six tails. She fanned them rapidly, and soon pink energy waves rippled out and slammed into the boat, rocking it.

More and more energy waves emanated from the aliens tail, until it began to jostle the boat so violently that the Coast Guard turned tail and tried to flee.

But that's not where it stopped. With a big whipping motion, Sayathong sent a giant energy wave hurling toward the lake. When it impacted the water it sent up an actual tidal wave. The wave only seemed to grow bigger and bigger as it went, forming a lip and then curled over as it rolled toward the Coast Guard's ship.

By the time it was bearing down upon them, the wave had turned into a thirty-foot tall tidal wave and slammed into the boat with the full force of a tsunami. The boat was crushed under the crashing wave and broke into a thousand fragments leaving nothing but drift wood and particle board. It wasn't so much sunk as it was completely demolished.

"Imagine, Travis, if one alien has the power to sink an entire boat and her crew, what do you think two thousand aliens might be capable of?"

"Two thousand?" I asked.

"Oh, you didn't know?" Dr. Castle smiled and gestured to the city. "Their numbers have tripled since our last encounter. You see, by giving them a steady dose of their blue atmosphere, they grow quickly. Faster than any land mammal on this planet. Not only that, but the blue gas that I've perfected not only strengthens them, but it enhances their psychic powers too. A quaint, but welcome side effect, I assure you."

"Travis, let's go," Megan said, tugging on my sleeve. "We've gotta leave before the rest of the military shows up." I nodded and turned to follow her back to the van.

"Hey, Travis," Dr. Castle said, calling out to me. I paused and looked back one last time. "Thanks for the warning. Oh, and keep the gun. You'll be needing it more than I."

With that, the doctor turned back toward the throng of aliens which parted to let him through. As he walked into their numbers, the wall slowly closed up behind him as they filed back into position.

Sayathong looked at me and I looked at her, our eyes meeting. "Good luck," I said.

Unable to prevent the coming battle, I got back in the van.

"What about Lucy?" Billy asked, as Megan and I got back into the vehicle and shut the doors.

"I'm afraid Lucy is on his own." I placed my hands on the steering wheel and tried to think of another way to warn Lucy, but nothing came to mind. It was clear that Sayathong and her ilk weren't going to let us continue into the city any further.

Not willing to risk anyone's lives for one alien, I shifted the car into gear, cranked the wheel and slowly turned to head back the way we'd come. To my surprise, standing in the middle of the road was Lucy.

Reflexively, I hit the brakes and brought us to a full stop and we all stared at Lucy who peered back through the Plymouth Voyager's cracked windshield at us.

"Speak of the Devil," Paul said, "and he shall appear."

"Boy, am I glad to see you." I pointed up, to the roof of the van, and Lucy seemed to understand the mission and climbed up onto the roof and wrapped a couple of his tails around the roof rack to help tether himself. With our resident alien tied down, I shifted the van into gear and floored it. With a whine and a rattle, the minivan gradually pulled away from the city.

Roughly two hours on the return trip, the van engine sputtered and then gave up the ghost. Stalling in the middle of the road, I said, "Well, that's that, I suppose."

We all got out and Lucy leaped off the top of the van and came over and nuzzled me. Then turned and nuzzled Megan too.

Megan laughed. "We missed you too, you big softie." She patted Lucy's head and then turned around to find Sarah standing ten feet away, her eyes glowing turquoise, her veins hot pink.

When they made eye contact Lucy stopped and stared at Sarah for the longest time then went up to her. Sarah leaned in and a pink spiral formed on her forehead as she touched heads with Lucy.

They stood before us, their foreheads pressed together for about a minute and a half, and then Sarah slowly drew back and turned towards us.

"What is it?" I asked.

"I don't know how to articulate everything he

showed me. But, in the simplest terms, he showed me that Dr. Castle is creating an army of telekinetic aliens, aliens loyal to him like Sayathong, to do his bidding. If he's allowed to continue building this army, Lucy is certain that this won't just be the end of Chicago. This will be the end of the world."

"But how accurate do you think these psychic prognostications are?" asked Paul. "Because, last time Lucy warned Travis about a dangerous person, that person was Jen."

"All right, so what's your point?" I asked.

"My point is that she's not at all dangerous. I mean, Jen's probably in more danger of getting knocked up with how often I see her and Jimmy slip away to get their freak on. But other than that, she's basically just a normal high school girl."

"See," Megan said, pointing at Paul. "That's what I've been trying to tell you all. Jen is a total scarlet!"

"You might say scarlet," Paul specified. "But I'd merely say promiscuous."

"Is there a difference?" I asked.

Paul shrugged. "I suppose the Devil is in the details."

"What's with you and the Devil thing lately?"

asked Billy. He put his hands on his hips and shot Paul a slightly worried look.

"Oh, haven't you heard?" Paul said, a sly grin forming on his face. "Hell is empty and all the Devils are here." Pausing, Paul took a deep breath, looked back at us, and pushed up his glasses. "Calling a woman a Scarlett comes from the Book of Revelation. Chapter seventeen verses one through six describes a 'Great Harlot' dressed in scarlet and purple. This Harlot, aka The Whore of Babylon, rode upon a giant beast with seven heads and ten horns. I supposed that's the difference."

Not waiting for a response, Paul stuffed his hands in his jacket pockets and began hiking up the highway, following the yellow dotted line toward Sturgeon Bay and our home away from home.

"Well, that was cryptic," Megan said.

I nodded. Honestly, I had no idea what had gotten into him. It wasn't like Paul to be cynical or uncharacteristically grim.

While we were all chatting, I looked over to see Sarah and Lucy communicating again. Their heads touching and emanating a bright pink ora.

"What are you two talking about now?" I asked.

"I was curious about what they ate."

Billy eyes lit up and he smiled. "So, what did he say?"

"They like fish," Sarah said. "But they are omnivores like us, so they can survive on a diet of plants including most fruits and vegetables. But grapes, like with dogs, are poisonous to them."

"You got all that from one mind-meld?" I asked.

Sarah nodded.

"Wow."

"Hey, you guys coming or what?" Paul asked, waiting up for us.

"Yeah," Billy said, "We're coming."

Although our home was still forty six miles away, we decided to walk it knowing we wouldn't get back till noon tomorrow. This was the plan, assuming we didn't run into any other unforeseen obstacles.

Half a mile up the road, a couple of headlights appeared on the horizon and the rumble of a Hemmy V8 could be heard. We all shared concerned looks as we moved to the side of the road to let the truck pass.

We hadn't seen hide nor hair of another human being in weeks, and usually other people turned out to be dangerous or plum insane. So, we weren't looking forward to having to deal with another human being.

"Should we warn them that the city is about to be ground zero for the biggest military campaign since the Bay of Pigs?" asked Paul.

"I think we should let this guy pass on by without so much as a wave hello," I said. I turned to Billy and shot him an inquisitive look. "What do you think, Billy?"

"I think we need that truck." Billy cocked his shotgun and stepped out into the middle of the road.

"Are you crazy?" Sarah asked, stepping toward him. "You'll get yourself run over."

Billy raised a hand, warning her to stand back. "I know what I'm doing," he reassured her.

The truck came around the bend and its headlights lit up Billy Bardemn, who stood in the middle of the street with a shotgun aimed at the driver's cabin.

Easing to a stop, the truck's engine idled and Billy shouted, "Get out of the vehicle and hand over the keys."

The truck idled some more, its engine softly

rumbling, but when it became clear there wasn't going to be any answer, Billy shot a warning shot into the sky and then pointed the gun at the pickup truck again.

"I asked you once. I won't aske twice. Step out of the vehicle and give me your keys."

The truck door opened and Billy held the shotgun steady, squinting into the headlights to try and make out the figure.

Before any of us could see the person's face, they spoke, addressing Billy.

"Is this the way mom raised you, Billy Bardem? As a Shanghai, highway hijacking bandit? Or, are you going to set that scatter gun down and give your brother a goddamn hug?"

Sarah was the first to piece it together and, in a stunned tone, gasped, "Marvin?"

Stepping into the light, Marvin William Bardem smiled at Sarah Lewis and said, "Hey, there Long Legs. Long time no see."

"Marv?" Billy said, tears instantly bursting forth from his eyes. He shoved the shotgun into my arms and dashed toward his brother.

Billy leaped into the air, Marvin literally having

to catch him and the two of them embrace, laughing and spinning until they were so dizzy that they both fell over.

Lying on the pavement in the middle of the road, Marvin reached over and messed up Billy's hair. "Miss me?"

Lending a helping hand, I helped them both up and smiled at Marvin.

"Holy smokes! Travis, is that you? You've gotten so big."

"I'm fifteen now."

"And a fine gentleman you've turned out to be, too."

"Hey, cowboy," Megan said, smiling at Marv.

He turned toward her and whistled. "Don't tell me you're chubby little Megan McIntrye? Because all I see is a full blooded, grown up woman standing before me."

"Oh, stop," Megan said, blushing and letting Marvin's charm wash over her.

"You must be Paul," Marv said, reaching out his hand. Paul shook it and Marv continued, saying, "We haven't met yet. But I heard a lot about you."

"You have?"

"Yep. Heard you were the smartest kid in all of Woodridge."

"I wouldn't say smartest," Paul said, showing a rare moment of self-deprecation. "But definitely top three."

Well, so much for the moment of self-deprecation, I thought.

Marvin grinned and punched Paul gently on the shoulder. "You bet, kid. You bet."

"How did you even find us?" asked Billy.

"I tracked Travis's mom, Emily, down. There was some mail in their house with this Wisconsin address. I thought it couldn't hurt to check it out."

"You drove all the way out to Wisconsin from Illinois?" Paul asked.

"Sure did, slugger." Answered Marv. Without skipping a beat, he continued on with his story. "When I got there, everything was dark, but the front doors swung open and your mom," he said looking right at me, "greeted me with a rifle and the same ultimatum my kid brother gave me just now... get out of the car or else. When she saw it was me, though, she threw down the gun and gave me the biggest bearhug of my life."

"I'm guessing she told you what we were up to and asked you to come save our sorry asses?" I asked.

"Something like that," Marv replied. "I believe the way she phrased it was, she needed to 'send in the calvary.'"

"Yup, that was definitely my mom."

"And, as you can clearly see," Marvin said. Raising his hands as if he were the prodigal son himself, he looked at everyone and said, "The calvary has arrived."

Billy and Marvin hugged again. Throwing his arm across his little brother's shoulders, Marvin looked over at us and asked, "So, you guys need a lift?"

When Lucy stepped into view from behind the van, Marv reeled back. His back up against the front grill of his pickup, he raised his hand. "Whoa, there!"

We all looked around, expecting to see something else entirely, forgetting that most people weren't' accustomed to seeing an alien casually hanging out with a group of teenage kids.

"Oh, him?" Billy, said. "He's harmless."

"He's actually saved our lives numerous times," I added.

Sarah then went over to Lucy, her veins lighting up hot pink, her eyes glowing turquoise. She touched her head against Lucy's and then smiled. Turning back toward Marv, her glowing abilities slowly dissipated. "Lucy here says 'hi'," she said.

"Lucy?" Marv asked, his voice still wavering with uncertainty. Then, pointing at his own face then Sarah's, he asked, "And, uh, were you just glowing a second ago?"

"Yeah," Sarah laughed, brushing back a tuft of blonde hair and tucking it behind her ear. "I guess I do that now."

"Uh, cool, cool, cool," Marv said in rapid succession."

"My sister, Melody, named the alien. Even though it's a him, technically speaking. But the name seems to fit, so that's just what we call him."

"She named him Lucy?"

"Yeah," I said.

Marv stood up, finding some courage to face the alien. But he still was hesitant. "Why?"

"Nobody knows," informed Paul. "Nobody knows why Melody does anything. You sort of just get used to it."

"I see," Marvin said, rubbing his chin. It was clear that we'd given him far too much information to process for the moment. Luckily, Megan laughed and then slapped a palm down onto Marv's shoulder, snapping him back into the present. "Don't worry though. Lucy will ride in back with us."

Paul, Megan, and I climbed into the pickup bed and settled in alongside Lucy, who took up nearly three quarters of the back all by himself. At the same time, Sarah Lewis sat up front, inside the cab, between Marv and Billy.

"Let's go home," Marv said, turning the keys and turning on the engine.

The truck came to life with a roar and then, back wheels peeling out and sending up a cloud of grey smoke, the truck did a U-turn and we headed back up the road.

TO BE CONTINUED IN:

THE LORDS OF SUMMER ENDGAME

"If you enjoyed this story, we would appreciate you writing a review. Thank you."

ABOUT THE AUTHOR

Tristan Vick is a multi-genre author specializing in science fiction, fantasy, and horror, and has also dabbled in mystery and suspense. He graduated from Montana State University with degrees in English Literature and Asian Cultural Studies and speaks fluent Japanese. He lives with his wife and three children in Japan. When he's not commuting on the train or teaching English, he spends his time reading, writing, binge-watching his favorite television shows, and eating sara-udon. In addition to being traditionally published, Tristan Vick continues to self-publish under his imprint, Regolith Publications, LLC, and Regolith Comics. His comic book series, The Astonishing Adventures of Alicia Carter & Robot, has sold over 10,000 copies in its first year of release. His other comic book works include Daughter of Wolves, The Profane, Blood & Chrome, The Viking Berserker Zarna, and Animal Woman.

ALSO BY TRISTAN VICK

▼ Available Now ▼

The Resurrection Saga
BITTEN: Resurrection
BITTEN 2: Land of the Rising Dead
BITTEN 3: Kingdom of the Living Dead

The Valandra Time Cycle
Valandra: The Winds of Time (Book 1)
Valandra: The Dragon Blade (Book 2)
Valandra: The Goddess of War (Book 3)

The Chronicles of Jegra:
Gladiatrix of the Galaxy (Book 1)
Imperatrix of the Galaxy (Book 2)
Destroyer of Galaxies (Book 3)
Galaxy Under Siege (Book 4)
Galaxy at War (Book 5)
A Song for the Galaxy (Book 6)

▼ Coming Soon ▼

The Profane (Novelization)

Visit Tristan Vick's author website at:

www.tristanvick.com

www.ingramcontent.com/pod-product-compliance
Lightning Source LLC
Chambersburg PA
CBHW070609310726
48982CB00001B/22